I0450892

A LION FOR A TOMB

FRIENDS IN HIGH PLACES 4:
IGNATIUS OF ANTIOCH

CORINNA TURNER

unSeen

Copyright © 2024 Corinna Turner

First published in 2024 by Unseen Books USA
An Imprint of Zephyr Publishing*

The right of Corinna Turner to be identified as the Author of the Work
has been asserted by her in accordance with the Copyright, Designs and
Patents Act 1988.

All rights reserved.
No part of this publication may be reproduced, stored in a retrieval
system, or transmitted in any form or by any means electronic,
mechanical, photocopying, recording or otherwise, without the prior
permission in writing of the copyright owner or, in the case of
reprographic production, only in accordance with the terms of licenses
issued by the Copyright Licensing Agency, and may not be otherwise
circulated in any form of binding or cover other than that in which it is
published and without a similar condition being imposed on the
subsequent purchaser.

Scripture texts in this work are taken from the *New American Bible,
revised edition* © 2010, 1991, 1986, 1970 Confraternity of Christian
Doctrine, Washington, D.C. and are used by permission of the copyright
owner. All Rights Reserved. No part of the New American Bible may be
reproduced in any form without permission in writing from the
copyright owner.

Quotes from the letters of St. Ignatius taken from *Ante-Nicene
Fathers*, Vol. 1. Edited by Alexander Roberts, James Donaldson, and A.
Cleveland Coxe. (Buffalo, NY: Christian Literature Publishing
Co., 1885.) Revised and modernized.

Cover Design: Corinna Turner

ISBN: 978-1-910806-30-2 (paperback)
Also available as an eBook

This is a work of fiction. All names, characters, places, incidents and
dialogues in this publication are products of the author's imagination or
are used fictitiously. Any resemblance to actual locales, events or
people, living or dead, is entirely coincidental.

* Zephyr Publishing, UK—Corinna Turner, T/A

PRAISE FOR CORINNA TURNER'S BOOKS

LIBERATION: nominated for the *Carnegie Medal Award 2016*
ELFLING: 1st prize, Teen Fiction, *CPA Book Awards 2019*

Corinna Turner was awarded the **St. Katherine Drexel Award** in **2022.**

PRAISE FOR *ELFLING*

I was instantly drawn in

EOIN COLFER, author of *Artemis Fowl* and former Children's Laureate of Ireland

PRAISE FOR *A LION FOR A TOMB*

I found A Lion for a Tomb *profoundly entertaining, enlightening and educational. My 15-year-old son read it aloud to his younger siblings who hung on every word.*

SARAH ROBSDOTTIR, two time Catholic Media Association Award winner & author of *Brave Water*

I loved this, start to finish. Fast read, beautifully written, relatable, with plenty of twists. Turner deftly weaves the wisdom and heroism of Ignatius into the modern life and struggles of teenage characters who are easy to care about and root for. I was immediately drawn into Raz and Daniel's world and friendship, and the strength of that friendship makes me want to keep reading again and again.

If anyone has ever wondered what Saints who lived thousands of years ago have to do with their own lives, this book answers in spades!

NANCY BECHEL, YA editor at CatholicReads.com

Every book in the Friends in High Places series weaves the life of a saint into the life of a modern teen. In A Lion for a Tomb, Corinna Turner tells the story of St. Ignatius of Antioch, making this early martyr a believable inspiration for a young man facing an incredibly difficult choice.

MARIE KEISER, Author of *Heaven's Hunter*

A Lion for a Tomb captivates readers.

ANDREA JO RODGERS, author of *Heaven-Sent Miracles and Rescues*

ALSO BY CORINNA TURNER:

CONTENTS

CHAPTER 1

Done! I read the last line of my Physics book and flip it closed, a satisfied grin stretching my mouth. Tonight's studying is finished. My parents didn't stop me from coming around twice a week to help Daniel out after he got sick again—but only on condition that I keep completely on schedule with studying for my exams. My dad even locked the garage at home where I keep all my tools and projects so I can't waste a moment tinkering with anything.

My name catches my eye, neatly written on a white label on the front of the book: Razim Sadiq. Man, I can't believe in only a month—16th May—we'll be writing our names on the actual *exam paper*. What with Daniel getting ill again just before Christmas, it feels like our big exams have snuck up on me while I was worrying whether my best mate was gonna make it to his seventeenth birthday.

I glance over my shoulder. Daniel's tucked up in his bed already, skin paler than ever, all thin and bald from the chemo, with Arnie the Ancient purring faithfully against his side. Daniel's had quite a good evening, though. Not too much puking. Thankfully, he's just had his very last chemo session—somewhat in the nick of time. He has a few weeks to revise—and I'll be glad to stop losing sleep.

He's still running his rosary beads slowly through his fingers. Even after I've read my way through most of that Physics book. He probably nodded off a few times. If he'd hurry up, I could help him with his revision before he grows too sleepy. He's gonna get 'special consideration' from the examiners because of his leukemia, but it will only help so much. We're both desperately hoping he can get good enough grades that his parents don't insist he stays back a year so he can re-take his exams next summer.

Pushing that grim thought from my mind—we've been best mates and classmates since kindergarten—I straighten my stack of revision books, pull the Chemistry one out—that's our first exam—and push the others to the back of Daniel's desk. *Oops.* I bend to retrieve the handful of leaflets and little cards I just knocked off. The top one catches my eye.

It's an icon-style image of an old guy with a long beard wearing a robe. Skin the same tawny mid-brown as my own, but hair and beard white with age. A lion crouches close on either side of the old man, their teeth

2

sunk into his flesh, blood spilling onto his white robe, but his expression holds nothing but peace and joy as he stares out at me. How did they get his little icon-face to radiate it like that?

I stare at the image for a while. Those lions are *eating* him. Why is he so happy? Something about him reminds me of...Daniel. When he gets talking about God, the way he often does these days. The way his face comes alive. The way his eyes glow. Scary and fascinating all at once. He's been like that for a year and a half, now, since he first got sick just after he turned fifteen. I'm kinda glad for him, in a way, 'cause it's helped him get through everything, but I still don't understand it.

This old bearded guy has the same intensity. Who is he? I turn the card over and my eyes widen at the sight of the writing on the back.

"This is Arabic!"

"Huh?" Daniel looks up from his rosary — or possibly another doze. "Oh, the Syrian refugees put some of those prayer cards in the church. I was hoping you could tell me who the saint is."

I snort. "You may have an inflated idea of my Arabic skills." But I can't help peering at the top line, clearly a name. I spell it out slowly.

"Agh...nat...yus..."

"Aghnatyus? Oh, and there are lions! I bet it's Ignatius of Antioch."

With this hint, I get through the second word much

faster. "Yeah, Aghnatyus Antakia."

"What does it say about him?"

I'm about to snort again and point out that being able to read Arabic letters and knowing the language are two totally different things, but then I grin and surreptitiously palm my phone from my pocket.

Daniel's staring vaguely up at the ceiling, stroking Arnie with his free hand and not paying attention. A few taps and I've called up a translation site. I scan the little prayer card and wait while the wheel spins. Then I read out the first two lines, with convincing *ums* and pauses to make it seem like I'm translating as I go:

SAINT IGNATIUS OF ANTIOCH
Bishop of Antioch from 69AD until his martyrdom c.108AD.
St. Ignatius is best known for his eagerness for martyrdom, as eloquently expressed in the seven letters he wrote while traveling from Syria to Rome for his execution.

My eyes skipping ahead of my mouth, I frown and stop at the end of the sentence, reluctant to read the rest to Daniel. When I glance around, his eyes are wide.

"Wow!" he exclaims. "Your Arabic is way better than I thought!"

Hah! I laugh and show him the phone. "Nope. But AnyLangNow.com's isn't bad."

He grins back. "Okay, you got me good. I *was*

surprised!"

"Do you want to revise now?"

He holds up his string of beads. "Nearly there. Then, yes."

With only a small sigh—I'm not sure he's missed a day with those beads since he got sick—I turn back to my phone. Yeah, judging by the quote marks, the rest of the text is something this Ignatius guy said or wrote, and it looks wild. As in, crazy-insane-wild.

For, although I am alive and well as I write this to you, I passionately yearn for my death. My Desire has been crucified; there is left in me no spark of fondness for worldly things, but living water wells up inside me and whispers, 'Come to the Father.'

Yeah, it reminds me far too much of Daniel in one of his morbid moods. Sometimes I feel like he's only trying so hard to beat this cancer for the sake of his parents and little sister; for me and Katie. Like he's not that bothered himself because he thinks God is so awesome he doesn't really mind dying and being with Him forever. It freaks me out, big time.

Is God awesome? Is God even *real*?

God *is* supposed to be *great*. The familiar phrase flits into my mind, reminding me of when I was little, before my sisters were even born, and my parents sometimes took Sayeed and me to the mosque as a family. Well, *Ammi* had to sit separately, of course.

5

I eye the prayer card again. The bearded guy looks a bit like the old imam from back then. I do remember him, very clearly. He was *so* kind. All us children loved him. He talked all the time about how great *Allah* was and how much He loved us and how we should always do good things for other people. I don't know why he left—moved away, got sick, died, who knows. I was too young to pay attention. The new imam talks about rules and not much else.

I try to push the thoughts away. The doctors are confident this second round of chemo has the cancer beat. Daniel just needs to build up his strength and he'll be back to normal.

Or as normal as he ever gets, nowadays.

CHAPTER 2

After only a little revision, Daniel's fallen so deeply asleep I reckon he's out for the night, now. Even Arnie's purr has given way to little-old-cat snores. I guess the periodic table would put Daniel out at the best of times. I glance at the piece of his 3D computer art hanging on the wall by the desk. He's not very into science—unlike me.

I put aside the Chemistry revision book and stretch out on my camp bed, checking my messages. Nothing from my mum, panicking about my exams and telling me I can't stay with Daniel this weekend after all. Good. We've got to celebrate the end of his chemo! Even if he's too tired to do much. And Sunday is a big deal for Daniel, what with it being Easter. Especially since he didn't get to go to several things at church this week that he really wanted to.

I have one message from our best friend Katie hoping Daniel's doing okay and saying she'll see us tomorrow and that's all. She's probably busy revising.

I text Katie back that Daniel had a good evening, then open an email alert. There's a hovercraft up for auction. Starting price... Huh. I sit up and follow the link. Wow, what a heap of scrap. A barn find. This is exactly what I've been looking out for! Could this one actually go cheap enough? I click 'watch,' then drool over the photos for a while, trying to see which parts might be okay, imagining it installed in the garage at home, all mine.

I've got an itch in the back of my brain, though. Despite my pulse-pounding excitement over the possible hovercraft, I soon find myself opening an internet browser and typing in 'Ignatius of Antioch.' Why was the guy so happy to die? Maybe it will help me understand Daniel. We were so close growing up, yet now, half the time, I don't feel like I understand him at all.

Okay, here's an account of Ignatius's martyrdom, written by those who were with him: Philo and Agathopus, and maybe Crocus. Weird names. Hmm, no, scholars argue about whether it's actually a totally original account. But the fact that it's simple and straight-forward, unembellished with legendary details—whatever that means—makes some of them think that it's genuine. Apparently.

I open the page, settle my head more comfortably on my pillow and start reading. So, the Roman emperor, Trajan, was persecuting the early Christians. Kind of like what's happening to Muslims in Myanmar, but across the entire Roman Empire. Ignatius was the bishop of Antioch, where Trajan was staying for the winter. Hoping to deflect the Emperor's attention from his flock, "the noble soldier of Christ"—that's what it says!—gave himself up and was taken before the Emperor...

+

A guy in a purple toga lounges on a golden chair, a fancy coronet on his head, scowling at the white-bearded old man who stands before the dais in between two Roman soldiers.

"And who is this evil wretch who so zealously transgresses our commands?" Purple Toga inquires pompously. "Who even persuades others to do the same, thus bringing them to a miserable end?"

The old man looks up at the man on the throne—the emperor of most of the known world—no trace of fear on his lined face. He stands almost erect, shoulders only slightly stooped with age. "Why do you call Theophorus evil? Do you not know that all demons and evil spirits have been banished from the servants of God? But it is true, in the eyes of all such spirits I am indeed a great evil, for I have Christ the King of heaven within me and that destroys all their plans."

The emperor's furious brows draw even more deeply together in the face of the old man's fearlessness. "And who," he demands, "is this Theophorus?"

"He who has Christ within his breast—a Christ-bearer—and one borne by Christ—Christ-borne."

The emperor looks down his nose at the old man. "Then, Ignatius, also known as Theophorus, I must have the gods in my mind, where they give me much better assistance in fighting my enemies!"

Ignatius shakes his shaggy white head, his face pinched with sadness. "You call the demons of the nations gods — they are not. There is but one God, who made heaven and earth and sea and all in them, and one Jesus Christ, the only-begotten Son of God, whose kingdom I hope to enjoy."

The emperor snorts. "The one crucified by Pontius Pilate? Him?"

Unmoved by the emperor's mockery, Ignatius stares up at him, his eyes shining as though his enthusiasm is about to burst from him in the form of light. "HE bore my sin upon that cross, casting down all the malice of the devil under the feet of we who carry Him in our hearts!"

The emperor shakes his head, his supercilious smile fading into a disgusted frown. He waves his hand in a commanding gesture. "We hereby order that this seditious madman, Ignatius, who claims that he carries inside him a crucified criminal, should be bound and taken to the great city of Rome, there to be thrown to the wild beasts" — his eyes stab viciously at the old man — "that he might serve some small use by gratifying the mob."

The old man shows no fear. In fact, his eyes glow more fiercely than before, like lasers in his wrinkled face. His hands rise heavenward. "O Lord, I thank you that you have honored me with this opportunity to love you perfectly!"

The soldiers seize his wrists and clasp iron manacles onto them, but he just smiles that radiant smile. "Oh, I thank you, Lord, that you honor me with these iron chains, just like your

10

Apostle Paul!"

Shaking their heads and exchanging derisive looks, the soldiers tug on the chains fastened to the shackles and lead the old man away.

With dignified steps, he walks meekly between them.

Still smiling.

CHAPTER 3

I come awake slowly, too sleepy to do anything but lie quietly, though I'm far too hot. I know I'm at Daniel's without even opening my eyes. That faint aroma of vomit will hang around this room for weeks, even now he's finished his treatment.

He made up for his good evening with a spectacular bout of vomiting at two AM that went on for over an hour. But it's Saturday. Neither of us need to jump up for anything.

I push back the covers and try to relax on my camp bed, hoping to nod off again. I was having a weird dream about a really obnoxious guy in a purple toga and some old version of Daniel who was winding him up...

No, it wasn't Daniel. He had brown skin just like mine...

The light glaring through my eyelids drags me further awake. I open my eyes. Yeah, sunlight strikes the windows, heating up the room, spilling through the crack in the curtains. Good. Daniel won't be up to going to the park yet, but we can revise in the garden.

I turn over, putting my back to the light, but something jabs me in the ribs. I yank my phone out from under me, sighing as sleep flees even further away.

Might as well check if Katie texted back. I swipe the phone on, but the page that comes up is about…

Oh. I was dreaming about Emperor Trajan and Ignatius of Antioch, wasn't I? Why do I always have such weird dreams? I thought us science geeks weren't supposed to be that imaginative.

Nothing from Katie, but I close the page about Ignatius of Antioch. Enough about some weird old man with a death wish who died almost two thousand years ago! Now Daniel's cancer-free, maybe he'll gradually go back to normal.

An icy little voice whispers that we don't know Daniel's cancer-free yet, won't know until they get the test results back in a week or two, but I push it away. They're about as sure as they can be without the results in their hands, right?

And what if it comes back yet again? The voice won't be silenced. *They don't think he could beat it a third time.*

I push the voice away once more. Oh yeah, the hovercraft! Excitement surging again, I swipe at my phone, wanting to take another look.

Daniel's stirring over in the bed. He pushes out his arms, stretching, then gasps, scrambling up into a sitting position, staring at something.

"What's wrong?" I try to leap up too fast and topple the camp bed for the millionth time, ending in a familiar heap on the floor, as glad as ever that the rest of the football team aren't here to see my klutzing.

No reply. He carries on staring at his covers, a slight hitch to his breathing.

I flounder up and hurry over. "Daniel? You okay?"

Oh, he's staring at *Arnie*. I hadn't even noticed the cat was there, he's lying so still. An icy jolt shudders down my spine. *So* still. I reach out hesitantly and touch the furry back—yank my hand away. Cold and stiff as a chicken about to go in the oven. He's *dead*.

Heck. My insides clench uncomfortably, my throat tightening. My parents don't like pets—Daniel's faithful little rescue cat is the closest I've ever come to having one of my own. Poor old Arnie. Poor *Daniel*.

"I'm...I'm really sorry." The words sound so awkward. I blurt, "He...he had such a great life with you, didn't he?"

I cringe inside. How's that going to make Daniel miss him less?

Daniel still says nothing. His face is pinched, his eyes wide. He looks so shocked. Should I go get his mum? But I don't want to just walk out and leave him with the dead cat.

"I always thought..." Daniel speaks at last, under his breath, as though to himself, "...always thought he'd be there at the end, asleep on my feet..."

14

A chill breath blows right through me. "There at the end?" My voice is loud and indignant, shattering the silence. "Daniel, Arnie was *ancient*! How could you possibly expect him to be"—my throat clenches and I choke the words out, my voice cracking slightly—"to be there when...when you're an old, old man! *Why are you talking nonsense?*"

Daniel's eyes finally move from the dead cat, rising to meet mine. Still too wide, but now making an attempt at his usual calm. "Yeah, Arnie was very old. I suppose...I suppose this isn't unexpected, really. Ignore me, I'm being silly." But his voice is too thin, shaking slightly.

I'm sorry I shouted at him, now—and kinda not, too. "It's not silly to be upset," I mutter. "It's just silly to—" I break off for a moment "—to *talk like that.*"

Like you'll never be an old, old man...

"Yes, it probably is." He gives a weak imitation of a smile, but his eyes stray back to Arnie. After a moment he reaches out and lays a hesitant hand on the cold, furry body. His expression...like he's looking at a ghost. Or in a mirror?

Furiously, I push the thought away. But from his face...that is how he feels, isn't it? For a year and half, death's been hovering at his shoulder like a surveillance drone, but this is the first time he's seen it this close...

But it shouldn't matter now. He's *better*.

I want to scream at him, shake him, anything to get that expression off his face. "I'll, uh, I'll go get your mum." I slide out of the room before I can lose it.

This was supposed to be such a happy day.

+

I drive the spade into the hole I'm digging at the bottom of the garden, stamping it in hard, then heaving out a big heap of earth. I add it carefully to the pile, then glance at Daniel. He's tucked-up inside his dormouse-pod, as Katie and I call that hanging garden seat of his, under strict orders from his mum not to help with the digging. Daniel's dad won't be home until late tonight so we're going to bury Arnie as soon as Katie arrives. She and her mum are spending Easter Day with her dad, so her mum's letting her come around for an hour this morning.

Daniel's little sister has hardly stopped crying since she got up. His mum finally took her back in the house, to give Daniel a break, I think. Yeah, he must be upset enough himself without having to comfort Clare all the time.

Daniel sits quietly, a thoughtful look on his face as he gazes into the large shoebox on his lap, occasionally stroking the soft fur inside it. The fact that he's prepared to touch the dead cat makes my skin crawl. Guess he's not afraid.

Or determined not to be...

Daniel, mate, why do you always have to be so *weird?*

I dig for a while longer, until the hole is nice and deep, then put down the spade and wipe sweat from my forehead. Daniel still sits there, too quiet.

"So, uh, Arnie was a good little cat," I say, trying to distract him. "Does he get to go to heaven?"

Oh no, why did I just say that? I sink onto the garden bench beside the hanging seat as Daniel struggles into a more upright position, looking out at me, a familiar spark of enthusiasm burning in his eyes.

"Oh, that's really interesting, actually. You see, no one is quite sure."

My eyebrows go up. "If cats go to heaven?"

"If *any* animals go *anywhere* when they die. Because they don't have immortal souls, only mortal ones."

I blink. "Huh? Mortal whats? *Souls?*"

"Yeah, everything living has a soul, right? People, animals, even trees, did you know that?"

"Nope. Isn't that Buddhism?"

"No, a soul is simply what makes a living thing what it is. As opposed to it being something else. But only people have immortal ones that last after they die. Animals, plants, their souls just go *pfft* or something."

I stare at him. "So...no animals in heaven?"

"Traditionally, it was assumed not. But the Church has never said for definite, which leaves people free to believe there could somehow be. Which a lot of people do believe, nowadays. Because we appreciate animals' unique personalities more than people used to and that makes us think they must survive in some form."

"Uh...and what do you think?" Have I just rubbed salt in his wounds? Though he's clearly delighted to talk about something this 'interesting.' I do *try* to listen when he gets going. Most of the time. Since our old friends cleared off when he got sick, he hasn't got many people to talk to. Just me and Katie. And the kids at his church youth group, I s'pose.

I avoid the really central stuff as much as I can. Like Jesus, AKA the prophet Isa. I mean, everyone knows not even the early Christians *actually* thought he was God, God's son, whatever. All that craziness. My brother Sayeed's hammered that into me—and my cousin Noora too, more gently. The errors all crept into Christianity later. But if I try to tell Daniel that... Well, we'd probably argue and what if I actually convinced him? I haven't anything better to offer him. Then he'd have to face all this with *nothing*.

He purses his lips and twists them sideways. "I'm really not sure. The traditional way of looking at it makes a lot of sense, and there is no getting around the fact animals don't have immortal souls. But I've heard a few good theories. For example, I read some theology graduate online suggesting that maybe there won't be *individual* cats and dogs but there will be, like, the essence of cat and essence of dog, that kinda thing."

"Like the master copy of a dog and cat?"

"Yeah. And Father Thomas pointed out that if everything is one Eternal Now to God, and everything exists in Him, held in being by Him, at every moment, then when we're in heaven, united to Him, our pets must be there, in some kinda way, because it's all *now* to God and they're in God like everything else. Probably not there quite the same way *we're* there, with our immortal souls. But existing. Make sense?"

I groan and put my head in my hands for a moment in protest. "Were you talking English?"

"Very funny, Raz." He eyes me closely as I raise my head again. "You understood just fine."

Yeah, we've talked about how everything takes place *now*, to God. And how everything, including each of us, would stop existing if God didn't hold us in his mind at every moment: *poof*. And how heaven means being totally united with God.

Yeah, I've heard enough about *that one*...

"Of course," Daniel adds, "people get very fixated on heaven, nowadays, and forget that heaven's only temporary, and we're all going to get our physical bodies back one day. So, some people think that there *won't* be animals in *heaven*, but that God can recreate our pets for us when He creates the new heavens and new earth, easy-peasy."

Allah can do anything, I suppose—if He exists—so that makes sense.

"You would not *believe* how much ink has been spilled over this, though." Daniel shakes his head, grinning. "*Man*, the discussions on social media...people get so fired up..."

"But what do *you* think?" 'Cause I'm getting curious, now.

He shakes his head again. "I think everyone's missing the point. Completely. Yeah, if I get to heaven

19

and Arnie runs over—metaphorically—and winds around my ankles, I'll be really happy, right? Of course I will. But if I get to heaven and Arnie doesn't run over and wind around my ankles, I'll be just as happy. Because, firstly, God is perfect justice, truth, and beauty, right? So if Arnie isn't there, that's the most just, true, and beautiful thing that could be, even if I can't understand how while I'm sitting right here, right now, with my puny mortal brain. I'll understand it *then*. And secondly...

"I mean, come on, *God!*" His face blazes with a depth of conviction I could never shake. "How could I be sitting around missing a created thing when I'm in the presence of God? I'll be radiantly, perfectly happy; totally complete. I won't need anyone or anything else to make me happy. Ever!"

His glowing eyes radiate excitement—joy—his earlier shakenness in the face of Arnie's still, cold corpse forgotten. His expression is so like that of little icon-Ignatius. How does he bubble with joy while talking about this? I don't even want to touch the dead cat, let alone think about dying myself. Or him dying... My stomach goes cold and funny just at the thought, my mind skittering away in practiced evasion. No wonder everyone gives him a wide berth.

I rub a hand over the stubble on my head—no need to shave it again in solidarity, now Daniel's finished his treatment—and sigh. Maybe I should read a bit more about Aghnatyus Antakia. See if he shares the secret.

Daniel-ese for beginners.

Yeah, why not. Worth a try, right?

CHAPTER 4

Daniel's soon napping, tired out by Pets In Heaven 101, so I find my phone and after checking on the hovercraft—no bids yet—I'm soon looking at one of Ignatius's actual letters. He wrote this—well, dictated it, apparently—to the church in Rome in 108AD, or thereabouts. Less than eighty years after Jesus/Isa got crucified, according to Daniel—or not, according to Sayeed and Noora.

Ignatius is believed to have been a student of the apostle John, a 'second generation Christian'. One tradition even thinks he was the child that Jesus held on his knee at one point. About as early a Christian as you can get. Which makes it kinda interesting, but can it really have any relevance to Daniel?

I start reading.

From Ignatius,
who is also called Theophorus,

To the Church which has obtained mercy,
through the majesty of the Most High Father,
and Jesus Christ, His only-begotten Son;

Immediately there's stuff about Jesus and how he's God's son. Maybe this isn't a good idea. Sayeed would flush my head down the toilet again if he knew I was reading Jesus-stuff. My big brother has almost Daniel-level enthusiasm for religion these days—but it hasn't made *him* nicer. Quite the opposite. Now when he beats up anyone who doesn't agree with him, he's totally self-righteous about it, thinks he's serving *Allah*. Who may not even exist...

But the thought of Sayeed sends a zap of defiance through me. And...hang on, God's *son*? But this was written too early for that, right? I bend my head to read on.

to the Church which is beloved and enlightened
by the will of Him that wills all things
which are according to the love of our God Jesus Christ...

I stop reading, my eyes fixed to the words 'our God Jesus Christ.' After a moment I scroll back to the top and double-check the introduction. The latest possible date for the letters is given as 117AD, though most scholars think that they and Ignatius's martyrdom were earlier, around 108AD.

So...the early Christians quite obviously *did* think of

Jesus as God, and God's son! They wouldn't have revered this bishop-guy who knew the apostles if he said crazy stuff they didn't believe in. Hah, Sayeed's wrong! I could shove this letter under his nose as proof... Yeah, and get a beating for my trouble. Maybe not. He is wrong, though!

I luxuriate in this delightful fact for a few more moments, then read on. There's almost immediately another reference to 'Jesus Christ, the Son of the Father.' And another to 'Jesus Christ our God.' Oh yeah, they totally believed that stuff. Why is Sayeed going around saying otherwise when there's hard proof? Someone must have told him it as a fact and he's just parroting it.

I read on, slowly, checking the explanatory notes regularly. So much of the ancient world stuff is strange, though a lot of the religious parts are somewhat familiar from conversations with Daniel.

Ignatius is so proud of his chains. He even calls his current situation — condemned to death and on route to his execution — as "an admirable beginning." Beginning of the end, more like!

No, the little prayer card wasn't lying about his eagerness. He *wants* his sentence to be carried out. *I shall I never have another such opportunity of getting to God*, he writes. And, *How good it is to be setting out from the world towards God, that I may rise again in His dawn!* Yeah, that sounds like Daniel-speak.

He's *very* anxious that the Roman Christians don't petition the authorities and get his sentence overturned:

I am writing to the Churches, to impress on them all that I am truly willing to die for God, unless you hinder me. I beseech you not to show such untimely goodwill towards me. Suffer me to become food for the wild beasts, for they can enable me to reach God. I am the wheat of God; let me be ground by the teeth of the wild beasts, that I may become the pure bread of Christ.

Whoa! That's... I dunno... Jesus sometimes appears as bread, that's one of the wackiest things Daniel keeps trying to explain. A sacrifice. Does Ignatius see himself as a sacrifice too?

A movement catches my eye. Katie has just come out of the house, her hair a golden veil in the sunlight. Seeing me bent over my phone, she approaches quietly, peeping into the dormouse-pod before settling on the bench with me.

"How is he?" she asks softly.

"Seemed shaken up first thing, but he bounced back pretty fast. Telling me all about the different theological arguments for whether pets go to heaven, just now."

Katie's whole face eases and lightens as she laughs. "He's okay, then."

"Yeah, I think so."

"I'm just sorry my 'congrats on finishing chemo gift' is now a 'sorry your cat died' gift."

"Yeah, the timing sucks."

"Poor old Arnie, he was such a softie." Katie sighs, then glances Daniel-wards again and brightens. "D'you think he'll be well enough for youth group on Saturday?"

"That's almost a week. Probably."

"Good. What are you reading?"

"Oh, uh...nothing important." I pocket my phone.

But it was important to Ignatius. And is to Daniel. So important I almost feel like I just lied. Even though it's not important to *me*.

+

Arnie's been laid to rest and we've had a little wake-slash-end-of-chemo celebration with cake and some "forbidden fizz" as Daniel calls it. Since he got sick his mum acts as though one sip or bite of something unhealthy and he might drop dead on the spot. Katie's hurried off home—her parents don't believe she can revise properly with other people around—as yet unaware (I hope) that I stuck two little truffle-filled Easter eggs—from Daniel and me—into her bag when she wasn't paying attention.

Daniel's mum has lured Clare away again. Daniel and I stay out in the garden, enjoying the sun, though I fetch our English revision books so we can test each other. We've got to do as much today as possible.

When Daniel dozes off, I carry on working for a while. But eventually I pick up my phone and swipe it on to read more of Ignatius's wacko letter.

He describes his journey from Syria to Rome, in the

company of "half-a-score of fierce leopards," AKA Roman soldiers, and then it just gets weirder and weirder.

Let no power, visible or invisible, grudge me that I should reach Jesus Christ. Let fire and the cross; packs of wild beasts; lacerations, breakings and dislocations of bones; cutting off of members; shattering of the whole body—let all the dreadful torments of the devil come upon me: only let me win through to Jesus Christ!

Near the end comes that extraordinary quote from the back of the prayer card. When I've finished the letter I stare at Daniel, who still sleeps curled up in his nest. The sheer...passion...of the letter has set my insides quivering. I feel like I've just accidentally closed a circuit and got an electric shock.

Is that how Daniel feels? If it is...it would make sense why he's so...so infuriatingly calm about it all, even the very worst possibilities. But is this Ignatius guy even sane? Why does he think he has to die like *that* to get to God? Don't all Christians go to God, however they die? Or believe that they do?

Martyrdom. Daniel talked about that a few months ago. Said it was a kind of shortcut. That it didn't matter what you'd done, or if you'd never believed until a moment before you died, if you laid down your life for God, you'd go straight to heaven. No purgatory. I s'pose that's kinda the same in Islam, except a martyr has to die fighting whereas for Christians it's the opposite. Maybe Ignatius doesn't have much faith in his own goodness and wants the certainty provided by martyrdom. Maybe it's just pragmatic?

He doesn't *sound* very pragmatic about it, though. What was that astonishing paragraph? I scroll back up a bit.

All the pleasures of the world, and all the kingdoms of this earth, shall profit me nothing. It is better for me to die on behalf of Jesus Christ, than to reign over all the ends of the earth. "For what shall a man profit, if he gain the whole world, but lose his own soul?" Him alone do I seek, who died for us: Him alone do I desire, who rose again for our sake.

The birth pangs are upon me; bear with me, brethren: do not bar me from living, do not wish for me to be stillborn. I desire to belong only to God; do not give me back to the world. Suffer me to reach pure light: only once I have shall I be a true man. Permit me to imitate the passion of my God.

If anyone has Him within himself, let him understand what I desire.

Re-reading it sets my insides jangling all over again, like my stomach's full of high tension cables and someone's twanging them like guitar strings.

Okay, I feel like...like maybe Ignatius has given me

an insight into how Daniel *feels*. But why? No, not why. I can see why, I s'pose. Because he loves God, and thinks God loves him back. But...?

I'm not even quite sure what I'm not sure about. But I am really, really confused. Death is the scariest thing there is. How do Daniel and Ignatius feel like this about it?

Okay, God's love.

But how do they know God's real?

Without knowing that, how do they... I mean...

How? Just...

How?

CHAPTER 5

An old man and ten brutal soldiers.

They toil along dusty roads.

They bob in a frighteningly small boat on a really large sea.

They trudge along more dusty trails.

They stop, now and then, in white-washed towns. Other bishops and their representatives travel forty miles or more to visit the white-bearded old man in his chains. In haste, he dictates letters for them to take away with them and send on to other communities.

And finally they reach Rome. Everything happens so fast. The games are almost over. The old man is rushed to the great arena. The bloodthirsty crowd bays for his blood. Wild beasts are released, unfed and ravenous...

Afterwards, his companions tenderly gather up his gnawed bones and send them back to Antioch. The persecution is over. And then the old man appears to many of them in a vision.

Still smiling...

"Something very bad is about to happen to my brain."

"Huh?" I jerk my lolling head up and try to pretend I wasn't doing a Daniel.

"My brain," repeats Daniel. "It's imminent. Something messy. Involving self-destruction. And goo."

"Charming." But I know how he feels. The sun is setting, but we're still poring over our books and questioning each other back and forth. I've let him sleep whenever he nodded off, but other than that I've kept us hard at it. I'm so afraid of him getting held back a year. Way better than him *dying*, but still.

"Don't you think it's time to call it a day? Unlike you, I don't remember things after reading or hearing them only once."

I almost say, no, we've got to keep going, despite the fact I'm dozing off myself. But there's a frail edge to his voice. Daniel's not a complainer—not since he got ill. He must be really tired.

"Remembering isn't everything. Still gotta apply it." Which I'm not so good at. "But, yeah, guess we need to stop soon. Even though you don't want to do *any* revision tomorrow."

Daniel gives me a look. "Don't start, Raz! It's Sunday, and *Easter Sunday*, at that. Six days to work, one to rest. We'll both do better on that than if we work every second."

"I really hope you're right. You don't have any time to waste."

31

"Time set aside for God isn't *wasted*."

"Yeah? Tell that to the examiners."

He changes the subject. "You want to come to youth group next week? First puke-free Saturday for weeks; I am definitely taking that night off."

I actually do want to go, quite a lot. I have for months. He and Katie talk about it all the time and it feels like there's a whole section of their lives, a whole group of their friends, who are closed off from me. But I'm really not interested in Jesus-stuff.

"We've just started on classic films set in Ancient Rome," Daniel goes on cheerfully, as though I haven't said no a hundred times before. "They watched *Ben Hur* last week, but that's the only one we've missed. It's *Spartacus* next Saturday, then *Quo Vadis* the following week."

I open my mouth to refuse, but he jumps in, "Pizza and a movie, Raz. It's the *social* night, that's all."

So he keeps saying, but I just can't quite believe this isn't a stealthy attempt of his to convert me. But...I've heard of *Spartacus*. And ancient Rome, that's where they're taking Ignatius to be lion food...

"I'll think about it." The words just pop from my mouth. *Aw, Razim, what are you doing? Getting his hopes up! You know you can't really go. Sayeed would —*

My thoughts skid to a halt, heat rushing into my cheeks. Because that's it, isn't it? Daniel talks about religion *all the time*. The real reason I won't go to a youth group held in a Catholic church hall is because I'm too scared of what Sayeed will do if he finds out. I just haven't been willing to admit it to myself. I did start standing up to him more for a while, a year or so back, after I grew a bit, but since my brief, unfulfilling attempt to practice our parents' faith, he's got so much worse that I try to keep a low profile these days. It winds him up enough that I'm friends with Daniel.

Let all the dreadful torments of the devil come upon me: only let me win through...

Heck, Ignatius wasn't afraid of *anything*. At all. Why can't I be that brave?

Why *can't* I? "Actually, uh, I think I will come this week." I speak in a rush, before I can chicken out.

Daniel pauses, his mouth half-open. His eyes light up. "You will? Fantastic! It'll be great, you'll see! We always have a blast."

I shrug. "Hey, man, I just can't resist the free pizza any longer, okay?"

He grins. "Fair enough."

CHAPTER 6

Easter Sunday dawns sunny again. Daniel's been anticipating today with great enthusiasm and not just for edible reasons. This time, he steamrollers his parents' attempt to get him to stay home from church, obediently donning a face mask to soothe his mum's nerves before flopping into the car. What he really wanted was to attend some super long service last night, but his mum put her foot down about *that*.

He leaves me with a large chocolate Easter egg to snack on while I do a bit more revision. I've got a big chocolate spaceship hidden in my backpack which I'll give him when he returns. Probably meant for kids, but I know he'll think it's fun. I'm guessing Katie gave his mum eggs for both of us when she came round yesterday and they'll appear at some point, so I can eat this whole egg while Daniel's out if I want to.

Most of all, I'm looking forward to lunch. Daniel's mum will do a first-rate roast dinner with pudding. My parents don't celebrate Easter, but they always let

Daniel have me around, yum!

After half an egg and only a few pages of my history book, I find myself googling Ignatius of Antioch again. They don't seem to know much about his life. He and another guy—Polycarp—were probably both disciples of the Apostle John and traveled with him to many cities (according to something called the 'Coptic synaxarion for St. Ignatius'). He became bishop of Antioch in AD69, roughly in his mid-thirties or early forties, only about thirty-five years after Jesus did or didn't die. He was most likely ordained bishop by John, although other sources say Peter or Paul. Someone major, anyway.

He loved music—huh, like Noora—at least, he mentions it in three of his letters, and according to an "Ecclesiastical History" by someone called Socrates Scholasticus, it was Ignatius who introduced something called 'antiphonal chanting' to the Christian Church after seeing a vision of angels hymning in alternate chants to the Holy Trinity. I wonder if Noora would find that interesting?

More likely she'd be worried that I was reading about a Christian saint.

Once arrested and on route to Rome, he wrote his famous seven letters. Four when the soldiers paused at Smyrna for a couple of days, three to churches in cities he wouldn't be visiting—Ephesus, Magnesia, and Tralles—plus the one he sent on ahead to the church in Rome to beg them not to save his life! Then he wrote three more from Troas—to churches he'd already visited in Philadelphia and Smyrna—plus a personal letter to his friend Polycarp, now the bishop of Smyrna.

Huh. The fact that he took the time to write a goodbye letter to his friend makes him seem far more…real…somehow. I mean, if someone told me I had to die, I bet I'd want to write a note to Daniel and to Katie telling them… What would I tell them? I'd thank Daniel for being my best friend since forever, I guess. And Katie?

My cheeks get hot at the thought of what I might tell Katie if the possibility of wrecking our friendship didn't matter anymore…

Hastily, I drag my mind back to my reading. From Smyrna, Ignatius was taken by ship, traveling onward to Rome via Philippi. But scholars don't agree on the initial route they took from Antioch to Smyrna. One possibility involves a lot of overland travel, but the martyrdom narrative says most of that section was traveled by ship. Basically, no one knows.

I'm not sure I'd like to travel on a ship wearing heavy metal chains. Although I guess it's a toss-up which is worse, being eaten or drowning. And walking all day with the chains rubbing must be super unpleasant too.

Ignatius almost certainly had to put up with some of both, anyway, because it's clear from his words in his letter to the Romans that he traveled overland part of the time. Apparently that wouldn't be usual if the soldiers' primary objective was simply to get him to Rome as fast as possible. Nor would it have been usual to rush one single prisoner to the capital, even a locally-prominent figure like a Christian bishop.

I suppose they couldn't just put him on a plane and have him there in a few hours. Travel was hard work, back then. So, the theory is that the soldiers must have been carrying out various other official tasks along the route, and they were just given Ignatius to take along with them. Makes sense.

In fact, it says Trajan probably sent him to Rome to die precisely to avoid giving him honor and fame among his local church. Huh. I guess that didn't work, since a bunch of them rushed to Rome ahead of him and witnessed his martyrdom anyway!

Apparently, it backfired on Trajan even worse because so many bishops and representatives from other churches traveled to meet him along the way, to encourage and to be encouraged by him. Which made him really famous. So the letters he wrote got circulated far and wide—especially after he got martyred so dramatically. Maybe, if they hadn't killed him, the letters would have just been lost. As it is...well, here I am googling them, almost two thousand years later!

Hmm, actually, the letters were sort of lost for a while. As in, some people added to them and enlarged them, kinda like ancient fan fiction, which led many scholars to dismiss the entire collection for a long time. But then, in the seventeenth century the original letters were rediscovered.

Oh, except for the letter to the Romans, which was regarded as a 'Martyrs' Manual,' and was always in constant circulation among Christians down the ages.

Huh. No prizes for guessing why. Just thinking about it gives me goose bumps.

+

I'm stumbling up a dark ramp in the midst of a press of sweaty, stinking bodies. My bare feet scuff against a hard stone floor. Ahead, eye-searing light pours down the tunnel as huge doors are opened. The bodies press me forwards.

Ragged breathing surrounds me. Over to my right, someone is sobbing. My skin crawls as my hairs stand on end, a suffocating dread gripping me.

At the top of the ramp, we're herded through the doors by Roman soldiers with uncaring eyes and sharp spears, finding ourselves in a massive arena—the Colosseum. The sand is bizarrely soft under my sore feet as the bloodthirsty roar of the huge crowd deafens us.

They've come to watch us die. They will enjoy it.

My stomach churns at the wrongness of it.

The last batch of prisoners are prodded through so fast, one of them careens into me and almost knocks me down.

"Careful, lad." Gnarled hands grip my arm, steadying me, and I look up into gentle nut-brown eyes in a wrinkled brown face.

Loud, coughing roars bring cold sweat to every pore. They're coming from gratings spaced around the high stone wall. How many lions and hungry beasts are in there? My heart's pounding so hard I expect it to…to break or something.

"I d-don't th-think I should b-be here…" I stammer.

"Not be here? Do not wish that, lad!" The old man slips an arm around me, his eyes shining with a radiant mix of love and longing. "Take heart; we will enter Glory together! Do you not know how eagerly the Lord awaits us?"

I wake with a terrible jolt. I'm lying in my own bed, soaked in clammy sweat, my heart aching with…with a strange echo of Ignatius's inexplicable desire. That was Ignatius, right?

Yeah. That was Ignatius. I really should stop reading his letters. I mean, now they're giving me nightmares!

At least I woke up before they let the lions out.

CHAPTER 7

"*Ammi*, is it okay if I go to Daniel's youth group tonight? We'll be having—" I bite off the word pizza just in time, since it's still *Ramadan*, and simply say, "a movie and hanging out."

Ammi may not pray much, but she still serves the evening meal after dusk during *Ramadan*—and won't let us snack beforehand, though she never asks us if we ate at school. I'm pretty sure she has a snack at lunchtime— Abbu too—because they're in no way cranky enough when they get home otherwise. *Ramadan* is definitely a cultural tradition rather than a spiritual practice, in our house. Except for Sayeed. So *Ammi* probably wouldn't be that bothered. But better not to make a thing about it.

"Are you completely on schedule for your exams?" she asks, peering at the screen of her laptop as she scrolls through groceries for her big *Eid* shop.

"Yes, *Ammi*."

Her mouse hovers between two varieties of

Tamarind chutney. "What time will you be back?"

"Before ten."

"Okay, then, *beta*. Have fun."

Yes! I grab my jacket from the hook and head down the hall, but Sayeed pops out of the dining room and dashes after me, grabbing my arm tight enough to hurt before I can quite get through the front door.

"There won't be food at this youth group, will there?" he demands. "You know it's still *Ramadan*."

I shrug, yank free and dart outside and down the garden path. Pizza. Yep. And I'm looking forward to it.

"There are over two hours of daylight left," Sayeed hisses after me. "You eat one bite, and you're gonna *burn!*"

Too late, bro, I ate lunch. And snacks. Lots of snacks. Every day.

Thankfully, Sayeed doesn't follow me.

I mean, I don't *object* to the idea of fasting. Daniel calls it 'a very helpful spiritual practice' and admires the way Muslims fast during *Ramadan*. *I* admire the way Noora fasts.

Be disciplined, like an athlete of God: the prize set before you is immortality and eternal life.

Yeah, Ignatius said that to Polycarp. If I believed like Daniel or Noora did, I'd fast, all right. Like training for football, but spiritual.

But fasting just for the sake of it? For something you don't believe in? No. That's almost a mockery, that is.

+

By the time I'm walking along the street towards Daniel's church, my heart is pounding in my chest. Am I really gonna do this? A church youth group?

But it's just a social. Daniel doesn't lie anymore.

Even those fleshly things that you do are spiritual, for you do all in Christ Jesus...

Yeah, in between school and revision, I've read another one of Ignatius's letters. The one to the Ephesians. Now I've got bits of it stuck in my head. With my exams coming up I love my excellent memory, but it has its downside.

And you should pray without ceasing for other men, for there is always hope that repentance may bring them to God ... and meet their violence with gentleness, taking care not to imitate their conduct.

With gentleness. I can't shake that bit from my mind. Sayeed likes to watch videos of would-be 'martyrs' chopping people's heads off. Real sick stuff. Not that I trust him for accurate information about religion, especially not since I started reading these letters and discovered he's *wrong*. If our old imam knew the stuff Sayeed watched, I bet he'd spank his bottom. Well, Sayeed's too big for that now... He tried to get Noora on board with his extremist stuff at the last family gathering and man, did she give him a piece of her mind!

Rejoice ... that in this worldly life you love nothing but

God.

Sayeed and Daniel would both agree about *that*. But... *With gentleness.* Ignatius even says that he is offering his life as a sacrifice. Not fighting. Just...offering it up. Peacefully.

There was a lot in the letter about the importance of finding God. *For let us either act in awe of His wrath to come, or accept His grace currently offered—one of the two. Only let us be found in Christ Jesus with our true life awaiting us.*

In other words, we can respond to either the carrot or the stick, just so long as we respond. But even assuming God is real, I'm not really clear *how* we're supposed to respond. What it actually looks like. Daniel, bouncing around with his eyes shining? What if you just don't feel like that? Katie, with her quieter dedication? Sayeed and Noora, praying in exactly the right way, five times a day?

It is better for a man to be silent and be, than to talk and not to be. It is good to teach, but only if he who speaks also acts the same way.

Daniel practices what he preaches, all the way. Katie just quietly gets on with it, like Noora. Sayeed talks far bigger than he acts. Claims we should all be out cutting infidels' heads off, then just beats up a few smaller kids now and then. He's always been a bully and a loudmouth.

Except...I glance around, swallowing, then bow my head and walk onwards. I s'pose I haven't wanted to

43

admit it to myself, how scared I am. I mean, after I refused to go with him to the mosque the third time...

I'm in the bathroom at home, Sayeed's knee grinding into the small of my back, my face plunged into the toilet, struggling to get free, struggling to breathe...I start to choke, to swallow water...he's not going to let me up! He's not going to, he's not, this is it...

I break free of the memory—wish I'd been able to break free from Sayeed so easily!—but my heart's pounding, sweat running down my back. Since then, I've tried to stay under his radar. Which is really hard when I live in the same house as him and my best friend's an 'infidel.'

Ammi and *Abbu* still believe he's their perfect firstborn son. It's sickening. Just because he hasn't been brought home in the back of a police car recently, they think he's not in a gang anymore. He totally is, he just changed the name from 'The Sick Kitties' to '*'aswad allah'*—The Lions of Allah—and now they're all into praying and watching those sick videos instead of roaming the streets doing graffiti. And when they do get up to something they make very sure not to be caught, 'cause who wants to go down for terrorism offenses?

There's the church ahead. I pause at the corner of the park opposite, eyeing the tall gothic building. People are coming down the steps in twos and threes, chatting and dispersing. Yeah, Daniel said there was a Mass at seven. Youth groups starts afterwards, at seven-thirty. About now.

The departing congregation are all so different. A young black lady in a smart suit, swinging a briefcase and talking on her phone as she gets into a taxi—gotta be a lawyer or high powered businesswoman. An older white guy in what's probably a janitor's uniform. A whole family with brown skin like mine, but they look more Middle Eastern than Pakistani. Could they be some of the Syrian refugees? A little old white lady, formally dressed, descending the steps slowly with her cane. An obvious down-and-out comes to help her—I can almost smell him from here. He just left the church too. A far eastern guy brushes past the two of them and hurries on without looking back.

What a mixed bag. But they all came.

For the beginning is faith, and the end is love; now these two, united, are God.

What the heck does that mean? The line has lodged itself in my brain so badly. Is it saying faith leads to love? So if I started believing in God, eventually I might be bouncing around like Daniel, overflowing with love? But how do you just start believing in a thing? Don't you need proof? But it also said, *He will appear before our faces, in so far as we justly love Him.* So love will prove everything, but one can't get the love without the faith? How does that even *work?*

The church towers high against the blue sky. According to Ignatius, that building holds *the medicine of immortality, and the antidote to keep us from death and make*

45

us live for ever in Christ Jesus. No wonder Daniel got so into it all.

Me, I'm just here for a free pizza, right?

Yeah. I'm so fed up of feeling left out. Sayeed probably won't find out, and even if he does...it's just a social. I'm gonna do it.

CHAPTER 7

Since I can't spot a church hall, I head up the steps and into the church, hoping Daniel will be there. I peer between the last departing worshippers. There! A familiar bald head in a front pew, bowed in prayer. Good.

I move that way, but a table covered in cards and leaflets catches my eye. I wonder...

I step over, my gaze scanning it quickly. *There!*

I pick up a copy of the Saint Ignatius prayer card. Are we allowed to just take them? I'm not a Christian, maybe I shouldn't...

Hey! I pick up another card. It's another icon-style picture, of the crucifixion. But the Jesus on the cross has brown skin.

"Hi, Razim, is it?" A deep voice speaks behind me.

I spin around, clutching the two cards guiltily. A priest towers behind me, black-robed, and...phew, a welcoming smile gleams in his dark-skinned face.

"Uh...hi. You must be Father Thomas."

"I am indeed. You're welcome to take those." He nods to the cards as though seeing my guilt.

"Oh, I wasn't... I mean, I don't want—" I break off, 'cause I kinda do want the Ignatius one. The guy still fascinates me. To cover my confusion, I thrust out the other card. "Is this *Jesus*?"

"Yep."

"Why's he got brown skin?"

"He was a Middle Eastern Jew. He most likely did have skin about...well, your shade."

Daniel might have said something about this, ages ago. "Then why is he always white?" I shoot a glance to the front of the church, where a massive cross hangs over the altar area, with—yes, a very white Jesus bleeding on it.

"Well, Jesus is God," says the priest, seeming unfazed by the question. "So although he did, specifically, choose to be born as a Middle Eastern Jewish man, people have always felt free to depict Him as their own race, to help them identify more closely with Him. White, Chinese, Native American, African, there's nothing wrong with depicting Jesus as any race if what you're trying to get across is the universality of God's Fatherhood to every nation."

"But?"

His eyes twinkle. "Yeah, there's a but. *But*, when European culture got exported to so many parts of the world so thoroughly, you now get the weird situation where sometimes Jesus is depicted as white even in non-white cultures. Because of this, some people think we should go back to strictly accurate depictions only. Others think ethnic depictions are fine, but need to be more strictly matched to the culture for which they are intended."

Huh, I bet Daniel loves chatting with this guy.

"So," the priest adds, pointing to the big crucifix, "British church, white majority population, white Jesus, fine." He points to the prayer card. "Syrian church, brown-skinned Jesus, also fine. But brown-skinned Jesus is the depiction that is always great everywhere, no question, because it's the accurate one."

Syrian? I turn the card over. Yep, more Arabic.

I look at the front of the card again. Brown-skinned Jesus stares out, very calmly, reminding me of Ignatius. Ignatius talked about *the cross, which is a stumbling-block to those who do not believe, but to us salvation and eternal life*.

Of course, Sayeed and Noora would say Isa was calm because He wasn't really going to die on there. But that always seems weird. Why would *Allah* pretend like that? Let everyone think Isa had died if it wasn't true?

I push the thoughts away. Free pizza. Movie. A few laughs. That's all I'm here for. "Uh, Daniel invited me to the youth group. Said it was a social?"

"Yep. Catechesis—religious instruction—is on Thursdays. It's just fun and food tonight. Do you want to wait for Daniel or shall I take you down and introduce you?"

Down? No wonder I couldn't spot the church hall. "Oh, I'll...I'll wait for Daniel."

"Righto. See you in a few minutes." The priest strides away in his long black robe, like a brawny grim reaper from a video game.

Daniel's still praying, no surprise. My eyes go back to that big crucifix hanging from its strong chains above him. It reminds me of Ignatius's letter where he called the Ephesians: *stones for the temple of the Father, prepared for God the Father to build with, and lifted up high by the crane of Christ Jesus — which is the cross — making use of the Holy Spirit as a rope, while your faith was the hoist by which you ascended, and your love the ramp which led up to God.*

I can't help picturing that sturdy crucifix there as part of some huge ancient building project, the chains as the cables, a wooden windlass... The Romans were technologically far ahead of their day.

Your love the ramp. Love again.

I'm still holding the prayer cards. With a wary glance around to see if anyone's watching, I slide them into my pocket. Both of them. A brown Jesus has serious novelty value, right?

+

The parish hall is underneath the church, accessible from the side of the entrance hall. Daniel walks carefully down the stairs, still not exactly brimming over with energy, but with a big grin on his face. Guess he wasn't sure I'd actually turn up. That makes two of us.

The hall is noisy, filled with way more teens than I was expecting, all ages. A few kids are setting out cups and plates on a table while a group of guys I've never seen before and one girl I recognize from our school's girls' rugby team move chairs and tables around.

To my left, a couple of kids our age are moaning about their parents and their revision and how they can't come next week. Ahead, some younger kids are talking about rugby. To my right, a couple of voices discuss something called 'atonement theory,' which I'm guessing is faith-stuff. But Daniel—and the priest—really were telling the truth. This is clearly a social gathering. Primarily for the church's teens, but still. It's just a social.

"Raz, you came!" Katie's already approaching us, her hair loose and tumbling around her face, which lights up as she smiles a greeting. Man, she just keeps getting prettier. I can see her and Daniel getting together someday soon. They both take their faith so seriously...

Pushing that thought away, I smile back. Then Daniel gets spotted.

"Daniel's back!"

For a few minutes everyone is surging around him and hugging him and patting him—gently—on the back, and someone starts a chant of "Daniel! Daniel! Daniel!" that turns him red as a sun-burned lobster. I stand like a lemon, but soon enough he distracts attention from himself by grabbing my arm and pulling me forward.

"This is Razim."

And then I'm being warmly welcomed too—"It's the Razzmatazz!"—like I haven't heard that before. Though one of the older boys insists on calling me "the imaginary friend," but only in a joking way. Guess Daniel and Katie have talked about me quite a lot.

The welcome-fest continues until Father Thomas sweeps in carrying a stack of pizza boxes.

"Pizza's here. Some of you go and get the rest of it, please."

When the pizza is all retrieved, there's a brief silence while Father Thomas says grace, then the boxes are opened and everyone talks at once as they get their pizza and drinks. Eventually the whole lot of us are settled and the lights are dimmed and the movie starts, projected onto the large white wall.

The film is old—and long!—but it seems no time at all before the credits roll.

"It was so sad when he had to kill what's-his-name," says one boy, as the music plays. "He thought of him as his son!"

"Katniss Everdeen could give them lessons on dealing with *that* situation," I can't help saying. "They should've just killed *each other*. Then neither of them would've had to suffer."

"Neither of them *had* to kill anyone," says Daniel firmly. "And neither of them should have done. 'Mercy' killing is false mercy. They gave evil exactly what it wanted."

"You really think they should've both just let themselves be crucified?" I demand.

He gives me that steady look. "No one says the right choice is always the easy one."

Everyone starts talking at once, then, but I can tell a lot of the kids here agree with Daniel, more or less.

No one says the right choice is always the easy one. Or like Ignatius wrote to Polycarp: *where the labor is great, the gain is all the more.*

Ignatius was certainly the king of doing what he thought was right, however hard.

"Real love," adds Daniel, meeting my gaze steadily, "isn't killing someone to take away their suffering. Real love is holding a basin of puke at three AM when all you want to do is sleep. If I haven't said it, Raz—thank you."

My cheeks heat up. "It's nothing," I mutter.

"That's not what I'd call it." Katie gives me such a warm look of approval I'm glad the room is dim 'cause there's no way my skin tone is dark enough to hide my blush.

Fortunately, people are getting up to go. "Goodbye" and "See you next week" fills the air. Daniel drops the subject in order to text his mum, and we go up to the entrance hall to wait for her to pick us up.

"That really was kinda a grim film," I say to Daniel, after Katie's mum has whisked her away.

"You don't think they should have stood up and

been true to themselves?"

"What good did it do? They all ended up dead. Horribly. Huh, ancient Rome was a nasty place."

"It certainly was for Christians and rebel slaves and anyone else who cheesed them off. I think they were brave."

"Brave, sure. But mad, too." Like Ignatius...

"How's the hovercraft doing?"

My mood lifts. "Still no bids! The auction doesn't finish until Thursday and I know it will probably shoot up at the end. But it's my best chance yet."

"Good. You've been saving up for ages."

A familiar car pulls up outside with a little toot of the horn so we hurry out.

Daniel's head is against the car window and he's asleep before we reach the first junction, leaving me alone with the image of a long, long line of crucified slaves who refused to submit to evil. Like Ignatius.

And some of the old lunatic's words, irritating ones that keep rattling around in my head.

And why do we not all have the prudence to accept the knowledge of God which we have been given, which is Jesus Christ? Why do we foolishly perish, not recognizing the gift which the Lord has in very truth sent to us?

What gift? Knowledge? Faith? Love? Or...an excruciating death?

Ignatius acted like that was a *gift*.

Yeah—thanks, but no thanks.

Why am I even reading this stuff?

CHAPTER 9

"*Ammi*, I'm going round to Daniel's to revise," I call into the kitchen.

"Does his mum know?"

"Yeah, we'll be in the garden."

As usual, Daniel's mum's gratitude that I stayed over two nights a week during Daniel's chemo to give her and his dad a break is already at war with her fear of him catching something before his immunity is all the way back up. He was really careful to talk about just how much he was looking forward to going back to his youth group *all the time* through chemo so his mum wouldn't have the heart to stop him.

"Can we come?" Dalal and Baheera peep around the lounge door.

"No, we're *revising*." *And you always end up fighting with Clare*, I add in my head as I head to the hall and let myself out. *And then all three of you cry and then it's somehow all Daniel and my fault.*

Uh-oh, Sayeed has slipped out behind me, closing

the front door firmly. Now what? He's super careful what he says around our parents and our little sisters so if he's trying to get me alone...

"Off to the infidel's again? You're really gonna burn, bro."

"A good Muslim lives at peace with everyone except during a time of war," I drone—as far as he's concerned, our parents are Muslim so that's what we are, too. I've given up trying to tell him that I'm *not*. To actually mean anything, religion *has* to be a free choice, surely? That's the one thing I am sure about.

He scowls. "Those verses were abrogated by the later ones, how many times do I have to tell you?"

I head down the garden path. "Plenty of scholars think differently," I shoot over my shoulder. So does Noora.

He's following me, a black scowl on his face, so I dodge across the road, through a tiny gap in the traffic. A bus honks at me, but Sayeed can't cross after me. Scowling harder than ever, he turns back towards the house.

You're gonna burn... It's my turn to scowl as I stride along. He nags *Ammi* and *Abbu* about not going to mosque—considering that they brush him off, they always seem bizarrely proud of how observant he is— but me? He just threatens me all the time, now.

These two choices are set before us, whispers Ignatius in my mind. *Death and life; and every one shall go to his own place.*

What, so Ignatius and Sayeed agree? Great.

I've been reading Ignatius's letter to the Magnesians and his letter to Polycarp this week. I meant to stop, but I can't quite help myself. The key to Daniel...to Katie...to *everything*? No, not the last. I don't believe that.

Right after Daniel got sick again, I video-called a lot with my cousin Noora—who's doing a GAP year in Pakistan—and learned how to pray right and tried it for a few weeks, even went to mosque with Sayeed. I just felt so...desperate. Desperate to do something for Daniel, desperate to...to have something to cling to, I guess. Like he does.

But the new imam just went on and on and on about rules, and Sayeed started following me around checking I was stepping into the bathroom with the correct foot first and that kinda thing, and as if that wasn't bad enough, *then* he started telling me how we should be killing infidels and how I couldn't be friends with Daniel anymore now I was a 'proper Muslim' and, whoa, suddenly I found out what a complete radical he'd become!

A couple of weeks of that, and I felt a hundred times worse. Daniel always says religion isn't about feelings, it's about faithfulness, and that's what Noora said too, so maybe if I could've made myself believe it, I'd have persisted. But I couldn't. So I decided whatever I was—an agnostic, probably—I wasn't a Muslim, and I stopped. Noora was really disappointed and so was Daniel. He thought it was better for me to get to know

God the Muslim-way than not to get to know him at all. Sayeed...well, he went totally psycho and almost drowned me.

Since then I've armed myself with Noora's best counter-arguments to Sayeed's arsenal of attacks for when I can't avoid him, and I've been trying to think about faith stuff as little as being best mates with Daniel will allow.

Do not let it seem to you reasonable and proper that you follow a private judgment of your own, whispers Ignatius.

But that doesn't help. It's not a matter of private judgment. The big problem is that there are, as far as I can see, two versions of Islam—Noora's more attractive peaceful one and Sayeed's very-much-not-peaceful one. It comes down to interpretation of the Quran. If the peaceful verses apply during times of peace and the warlike ones only during times of war, then everyone can live in harmony, like our old imam taught. But if— like Sayeed insists—all those peaceful verses, written earlier, were superseded by the later, warlike ones...

That's not good.

Noora would give me a lecture if she knew I was even thinking that Sayeed might be a proper Muslim— but how am I supposed to know?

+

The sun's dropping as Daniel and I go over our Chemistry yet again. I watch the shadows lengthening as I try to keep my mind on the different kinds of chemical reactions, but thoughts of the conversation I need to have with my parents about the hovercraft keep sneaking into my mind. And even more troublesome things...

"How do Christians decide which bits of the Bible are valid?" The words slip out at last.

"Valid?" Daniel stares at me, clearly startled that *I've* initiated a conversation about religion. "Well, it's all *valid.*"

"None of it, like, abrogates earlier bits?"

"Not exactly. The Old Testament has to be read in the light of the New Testament. Jesus instituted a far more radical law of forgiveness than people were expected to follow before he came, back when God made more allowances for how...well, how hopeless humans are."

Hopeless? What did Ignatius say? *Let us not, therefore, be insensible to His kindness. For were He to reward us according to our works, we should cease to be.*

Daniel's continuing, "So, sometimes the New Testament will mean that an Old Testament rule shouldn't be followed. Like, stoning people, for example. Doesn't line up with what Jesus taught. But I'd never say any of it isn't *valid*, exactly. Even laws on stoning teach us something about right and wrong, even if we'd no longer dream of applying them *literally.*"

"Huh." So Christianity is like Sayeed's version of Quranic interpretation—but backwards? Peace abrogating war? "So, who gets to say which bits to follow or not?"

"Well, for Catholics, the Church does. Scripture, the Church, and Tradition, the three pillars of the faith. A three-legged stool is very stable. If you cut any of the legs off, the way some Protestant groups kinda accidentally do, sooner or later things tend to get rather wobbly. But the Church has a hierarchical structure that safeguards the truth. As opposed to everyone just deciding for themselves what to believe. Which leads to chaos and is totally incompatible with the idea of objective truth."

Objective truth. The idea that something simply is, in and of itself, true, an unchangeable fact. Daniel's talked about that before. He obviously thinks it's very important, and I guess it is. Imagine if every electrician took a wiring diagram and simply interpreted it the way they wanted. It just wouldn't work. The diagram means what it means.

And…*hierarchical.* Ignatius talks a lot in his letter to the Magnesians about the importance of being united with your bishop rather than doing your own thing. The idea of hierarchy safeguarding truth is clearly something Christians have believed since forever. Catholics, anyway. I guess Protestants don't consider it so important.

"So…are Christians allowed to fight, or aren't they?" I'm getting quite confused about that.

Daniel's eyes light up with enthusiasm. Oh yeah, he can answer the question, probably in more detail than I want!

"Christians are permitted self-defense. And also national defense, like, if your country is attacked, it's okay to defend it. But Catholics have something called Just War theory that says that a war has to meet certain criteria to be acceptable—total war is never okay. Like, there has to be a reasonable hope of success, and you can't target innocents, you have to care for the wounded, the force used can't be disproportionate, that kinda thing."

"Of course"—his lip twists grimly—"some people argue that war is now so destructive, with modern weapons, that it's never justified. But that's a matter of personal opinion. The Church simply sets out the framework for discernment."

Hmm. Doesn't sound so different from proper Islam. Or what I hope is proper Islam. I assume he's finished but, no, he's raising one finger, looking more enthusiastic than ever.

"*But*, peace has always been hugely important in Christianity. Jesus offered his life without fighting, and the early Christians never fought back, either. Martyrs down the ages have imitated him by embracing non-violence, no matter the cost to themselves—many times even when it would have been perfectly acceptable to defend themselves."

His eyes shine with enthusiasm as he goes on, "They had a really deep belief—just like the early Church—in the redemptive nature of suffering and they saw accepting persecution and submitting to authority—however unjust—as an act of faith: faith that it was God who would heal the bad in the world, not any human effort. They would try to avoid persecution, they would even resist it non-violently, like when St. Paul appealed to be judged by Caesar, but, ultimately, if that failed, they would accept it as God's will for them."

"They'd just let themselves be killed?"

Daniel nods firmly. "Even nowadays, a majority of those called to imitate Christ most closely—priests and religious; you know, monks and nuns and such—would never consider it appropriate to fight for any reason. So yes, Christians are *allowed* to defend themselves, but to put your life—the world, even—in God's hands, practice radical love for your enemy and not harm them, no matter the provocation, is also something highly admired."

I frown, trying to wrap my head around this. So they are allowed—but they think not doing can also be a good thing?

"Wouldn't you defend yourself?" I ask.

He shrugs his thin shoulders. "I think I'd want to imitate Jesus as closely as I could if I was attacked and not fight back. If I was actually brave enough to do it— if I had enough faith in God's providence. But if a group of innocent people were being attacked, I think I would have to do something."

"I should think so!" I protest. "I guess it's up to you if it's, well, just you. But if someone else is in danger, you've gotta do something!"

"That's the norm, yeah," Daniel agrees. "But sometimes I do wonder what would happen if every Christian *actually* embraced total non-violence. Would that lead the *whole world* to convert and be at peace? But we just keep failing to trust and do it? Except"—he gives a self-deprecating shrug—"well, human nature *is* fallen, so I suppose it *isn't* ever going to happen. It's hard to see defending innocents as anything other than good."

A wistful expression crosses his face. "Don't get me wrong, I can see that total pacifism calls for a really profound depth of faith. I mean, how strong do you have to be to do nothing even when innocents or those you love are in danger? The way the early Christians did during the persecutions? What an amazing trust! I don't see that as bad, or wrong. Just...rare."

Daniel's yearning for what he sees as greater faith calls Ignatius' words to mind: *For although I desire to suffer martyrdom, I know not if I will be deemed worthy to do so.*

Yeah, I've been reading the mad old bishop's letter to the Trallians.

But after a moment's silence, Daniel goes on, "That level of trust in God...it feels like something we don't even...even *aspire* to, anymore, as a Church, as individuals, even. Which bothers me a bit, I suppose. And yet, letting innocents die...I find it hard to imagine myself *doing* it, and it feeling right. Maybe my faith isn't strong enough—or maybe it's something that certain people are called to only in certain situations, and usually the right to protect the innocent is paramount."

He shrugs again. "I think it's a God-level question, ultimately. Though I would note that plenty of groups of persecuted Christians around the world *don't* fight back, even nowadays. They choose to submit to the unjust laws of a worldly authority because they have absolute faith that God will win in the end, no matter what."

There hasn't been a suggestion of either Ignatius or the other Christians fighting back against Trajan's persecution in any of the letters I've read so far. This passion for non-violence clearly goes back a very long way. Another quote from Ignatius to Polycarp—his fellow bishop friend who also died a martyr—forces its way into my mind:

Stand firm, as does an anvil under the hammer. It is the part of a true victor to sustain injuries, and yet to end victorious. We ought to bear all things, especially when it is for the sake of God, that He also may bear with us.

Early Christians aspired to be the *anvil*—not the hammer. That is...radical. A different kind of radical.

"So....is martyrdom an...an honor or...just something that has to be endured faithfully?" I demand.

Daniel thinks about that for a moment. "I think it

depends a lot on how the person accepts it. But the early Christians, they would have seen it as an honor. Take Ignatius of Antioch, for example. He didn't think that the *Emperor* had chosen him to die. He thought that *God* had chosen him, chosen him to imitate Christ, to become a sacrifice. He definitely saw it as an honor."

Too right. *As I bear about these chains which make me worthy of the most honorable of all names,* Ignatius wrote to the Magnesians, *I sing praise to the churches.* He even said: *I bear my chains about with me like spiritual pearls.*

Has the prayer card inspired Daniel to read Ignatius's letters too? Probably. I'd love to talk to him about them—but I don't want him to know I'm reading them. I'm not really sure why. I guess it might get his hopes up that I was gonna become Christian or something crazy like that. Which I'm totally not.

I'm just trying to get inside *his* head.

CHAPTER 10

"And the auction's finishing at nine-thirty tonight," I finish, sitting tensely on the sofa in front of *Ammi* and *Abbu*. We've finished dinner, and I've just asked to speak to them and told them all about the hovercraft. "Please may I bid from one of your accounts?" They've never allowed any of us to have our own accounts on auction sites.

"Your exams—" *Ammi* says immediately.

"*Abbu* can collect it, it can go straight in the garage; I don't have to even touch it until after my last exam."

"Will you promise me that you won't, *beta*?" She gives me a super-serious look. "That you *literally* will not put one hand on it?"

"Yes. I promise. Not one finger, I swear. The garage is locked, anyway!"

Abbu gives me a shrewd look. "And will you promise you won't spend any time online looking up parts and how-to guides?

Eurgh. "Yes. I promise. I'm not gonna mess up my exams, I swear. But just imagine, *Abbu, Ammi,* when I'm applying to engineering courses or electrical apprenticeships, if I can show a portfolio documenting the complete restoration of a hovercraft! It's a fantastic opportunity."

They exchange a long, long look. I can hardly make myself breath. Finally, Abbu looks at me again.

"All right. You may use my account to bid. But you must not go one penny over what you can afford. I will drive the thirty miles and tow the contraption home if you win it, but we're not paying for it."

"Of course." My heart pounds with excitement. Might this really happen? I've loved hovercrafts for years, and I've been working towards owning a full-size one ever since that crazy dream I had during Daniel's first chemo. "I would never bid over!"

"Okay." Abbu glances at the clock—almost nine-fifteen. "I will log into my account—"

"Seriously?" Sayeed suddenly looms in the doorway—he's clearly been listening from the hall. "He hasn't kept Ramadan *at all*—and you're rewarding him! And worse, Maliq saw him going into a *church* on Saturday evening. A *church, Abbu!*"

Ammi and *Abbu* look from Sayeed to me, frowning. My heart pounds. Heck, why did Maliq have to see me? I know if I hesitate or act guilty, I can kiss that hovercraft goodbye—and the youth group, too.

"Yeah, the youth group's held in the church hall," I

68

say casually. "The entrance is in the church foyer."

"I thought you said it was a social club, Razim." *Abbu* is looking at me very closely indeed, and using my name. Uh-oh.

"It is." I force myself to speak calmly, as though I've nothing to hide. Which I haven't. "It's a normal Hollywood movie with pizza. They just happen to use the church hall."

Abbu and *Ammi* exchange looks. Why do they even *care*, considering...? But it's not looking good... I grope for something more to say and find myself offering the truth. "It's the social club for the kids at the church, primarily. Like Daniel and Katie. But anyone's welcome. Gives teens something to do other than hang around and, I don't know, vandalize a bus shelter now and then."

Ammi and *Abbu*'s eyes dart to Sayeed and their expressions grow more thoughtful. Yes! Point to me. They've always liked Daniel, made no secret of the fact that they don't think any friend of his is going to be brought home in a police car for damaging public property. Unlike my big bro.

Abbu's opening his mouth again. I try not to hold my breath.

"If it's not religious...I suppose there's no harm in you going." He glances at the clock. "I'd better log into that account for you."

Sayeed gives me a death glare, then spins around and storms away.

69

As I settle myself in front of the computer, *Ammi* and *Abbu* hang around, looking over my shoulder. Good. If they leave the room, Sayeed will probably come in and mess up the internet router at the critical moment.

I open the site and find the listing. My heart lurches. Two bids, now... It's at two hundred and fifty pounds. But it's still well within what I can afford. How much will it shoot up at the last minute? I've got six hundred and thirty two pounds painstakingly saved up from paper rounds and odd jobs fixing things. Will it be enough? A working hovercraft—or even a better conditioned spares or repairs one—is worth thousands.

"It's ever so rusty, *beta*," says *Ammi*, peering at the pictures. "Are you sure you can fix it?"

Smothering a pang of hurt—she's usually so proud of my skills—I reply calmly, "The frame is sound. That metal isn't a type that rusts. The rest...I just need to take everything to pieces and clean it and save up for each thing that needs replacing, one part at a time. And eventually I'll have a fully working hovercraft."

Ammi makes an 'if you say so, *beta*' noise in her throat.

Abbu also peers doubtfully. But all he says, is, "Razim knows all about these contraptions, I suppose."

There are three minutes left. I open the bidding window and get ready.

One minute... A bid comes in—it leaps up to three-sixty. A few seconds later, it goes up to four-ten. *Ugh,*

Ignatius, help! Nah, he's not going to help. He scorned worldly things, right?

Then again, Daniel seems to think that Jesus cares about everything in our lives, not just when we pray. I should've asked who the patron saint of hovercrafts is!

In my mind, Brown Jesus's calm face looks out at me from the cross. The cross where he's dying in agony. My hand strays to my pocket, where the prayer card is still hidden. Could he really care whether I get this hovercraft or not?

The price leaps up to five-sixty. Uh-oh.

Daniel cares. He's waiting anxiously tonight to hear if I win it. Even though he's also waiting for that letter with his test results, the letter that will tell him if he's gonna live or die...

Huh. Guilt and superstitious fear collide in my stomach. What if I get the hovercraft...but lose Daniel?

Uh...hey, Jesus, listen, if it's the hovercraft or Daniel, I choose Daniel every time. Just so we're completely clear on that...

Oh no, thirty seconds and it's at...six-ten!

I carefully type in six hundred and thirty-two pounds. All or nothing. I've been watching for months and there hasn't been anything else I was even close to affording.

Fifteen seconds.

My mouse hovers over the 'bid' button. My mouth is dry.

Ten seconds.

71

Six twenty-five...

Five seconds...

I click.

By the time the page refreshes, the auction is over, and the 'establishing the winner' message is showing. It must be close. My heart pounds heavily in my chest. Is it me? Could it be me? It was so close to my limit...

The page refreshes.

Congratulations. You are the winner.
£629

I draw in a massive breath, swept with a wave of relief—and belated anxiety. All my savings. I *really* hope it's worth it!

"Well," says Abbu, "it will be a good project for you, you're right about that. See if you can arrange for me to collect it on Saturday."

He claps me on the shoulder and they both move away.

I stare at the listing for a while longer, fear and excitement turning cartwheels in my stomach. My phone buzzes. A text from Daniel.

Was that your dad's account?

I text back: Yes. I won!!!! :D

The reply comes at once: Go, Raz! Hurry up and

fix it—can't wait for a ride.

I grin. Well, *he* assumes I can fix it, at least.

Only when I put the phone down again do I realize exactly what just happened back then. I prayed, right? That would count as a prayer. To *Jesus*...

What the heck, *Razim?*

CHAPTER 11

It's a rainy Saturday, but Daniel's mum has calmed down enough by now to let us revise inside. Daniel's room still seems quiet without Arnie, despite the fact all he did was lie around and sleep most of the time.

"Are you coming to the youth group tonight?" Daniel asks, as we finish a round of French flash cards.

"Yep. My parents are cool with it. Seem to think it will keep me out of trouble."

"That's great." He hesitates, flicking a card nervously. "Uh...I don't really want to say this, 'cause it was so great having you there last week, but... I know I should. *Quo Vadis*—that's what we're watching tonight—it was a really big budget Hollywood movie of its day, right? Big hit, too, saved MGM from bankruptcy. But Christian persecution in Ancient Rome is a major part of the plot, so it is quite religious."

He eyes me anxiously. Christian persecution in Rome? Like what happened to Ignatius...that actually really makes me want to see it, just at the moment. But I play it cool, shrugging.

"Oh, if it was a Hollywood movie, I'm sure it's fine."

He relaxes, grinning. "Great." He tosses the cards down and springs to his feet. "I need more snacks before I can read one more French word. Can you shuffle them?"

He dashes off to the kitchen. I pick up the French flashcards and mix them up thoroughly, then grab my phone, checking for messages. *Abbu* should be setting off to Surrey any time now, to collect my hovercraft. The seller had the sense to stick some new tires on the hovercraft's trailer before putting it up for sale, so that it would be roadworthy. All *Abbu* has to do is hitch it up to the tow bar and bring it back.

But I have to stay here and revise. Because I double-promised I wouldn't let it distract me *at all*...

Daniel comes back in. Did he forget the snacks? He's got a really odd expression on his face. *Wait*...he's holding a piece of paper in one hand, an envelope in the other. A type of envelope I recognize...

I cross the room in one bound and snatch the letter from his shaking hand, unable to wait for him to tell me what it says...

+

Curiosity kills cats, they say. Then again, Arnie wasn't the least bit curious and he still died. Everyone dies. I wish I could forget that fact. Go back to how I was before Daniel got ill. When death was so far away it was something that would never affect me. Or even back to before Sayeed almost drowned me. When death was just something that lurked around fragile Daniel, but still had nothing to do with strong, healthy me.

Now, every so often, the thoughts escape that box in my mind where I try to keep them locked, filling my stomach with that horrible panicky feeling of dread. I'm not immortal. I'm just as vulnerable as Daniel...

I suppose that's why I'm here. Because I'm so curious to see *the medicine of immortality, and the antidote to prevent us from dying, by which we live forever in Jesus Christ.* I can't deny that curiosity anymore, especially not now, when the uncertainty that has dogged the future for months has finally eased a bit.

I lurk at the back of the church, skin crawling with self-consciousness, unsure when to stand, to kneel... watching. Watching as Father Thomas, dressed in beautifully embroidered robes, stands at the altar, offering bread and wine to God. Or offering Jesus to God?

It's kinda beautiful, but I don't understand everything that's happening. But it reminds me of Ignatius telling the Trallians:

> *Therefore, arming yourselves with gentleness, be renewed in your faith (that is the flesh of the Lord) and in your love (that is the blood of Christ Jesus).*

Faith and love again, huh? And gentleness...

Soon everyone is walking up the aisle in a line and receiving something from Father Thomas. Bread? Or Jesus? Well, not everyone. A few people stay in the pews, so I don't feel too awkward about staying put as well. I eye the 'Son of God' there on his crucifix, looking down at everyone.

By the Cross, Ignatius said, *He calls you through His passion, being, as you are, parts of His Body.*

Is everyone here part of God's body...except me? I spotted Daniel's bald head at the front almost as soon as I came in. He's grown so much in the last year, almost as tall as me, now.

How can I know what is true? Could Jesus have really died? Not only died, but been resurrected? Could he really be...God's son?

Ridiculously, it's Aragorn who answers me, in Viggo Mortenson's soft voice: *What does your heart tell you?*

It's getting harder and harder to ignore what my heart is telling me. What it's *screaming* at me...

But faith isn't just about feelings. I can't act on feelings. I don't dare. What does my *reason* tell me? How can I reverse-engineer this? Find some evidence?

Ignatius says to the Trallians: *Some that reject God— that is, those without faith—say that He only appeared to suffer ... if so, then why am I in chains? Why do I pray that I may be thrown to the wild beasts? Am I giving up my life in vain? Am I not then guilty of bearing false witness about the Lord?*

77

Ignatius knew John, and maybe Peter and Paul, as well. John and Peter knew Jesus personally, right? What does Ignatius say in his letter to the bizarrely-named Smyrnaeans?

Jesus came to those who were with Peter and said to them, "Lay hold and touch Me, and see that I am not an incorporeal spirit." And as soon as they touched Him, they believed, being convinced both by His flesh and spirit. For this reason they came by their disdain of death, and so became its conquerors.

Conquerors of death. They were all martyred, right? Well, I'm not so sure about John. But Peter and Paul and Ignatius and all the other apostles who'd known Jesus...they all allowed themselves to be killed, that's how strongly they believed that what they were teaching was true.

Oh...the Mass seems to be over. Father Thomas has just walked out in a dignified manner, attended by two younger teens in robes, holding lighted candles in large candlesticks. Some people kneel to pray, others get up to leave.

I slip out into the foyer to wait for Daniel. I don't think he saw me in there, and I'd rather keep it that way.

I browse the prayer card table as I wait. There's a whole rack of leaflets with interesting/alarming titles such as 'What happens when we die?' and 'What is

Purgatory?' along with slightly more cheerful titles like: 'How do I get confirmed?' And 'Does God really love me?' My fingers itch to collect a bunch, but how would I explain them to Daniel? Let alone my parents. I put on one of my newest pairs of jeans and they've got such silly little pockets, I even had to leave my pair of prayer cards tucked inside my desk drawer for safe keeping.

Ah, good. Here's Daniel...

As we go down the stairs, he pulls out that letter again.

"Hey, guys." He waves the envelope as soon as we enter the parish hall, getting everyone's attention. "Uh... so, my results came."

Instant, deathly silence.

He draws the letter from the envelope, solemn-faced. "Yeah, so, uh, some of you may consider this bad news, but..." —he unfolds it and holds it up—"well, you're all gonna have to put up with me being around for a bit longer."

For a moment, confusion reigns, then an older boy—Francis?—grabs the letter and scans it. *"Leukemia in remission!"* He folds it and swats at Daniel. "You little monster, you had us all worried!"

Daniel laughs, but the sound is drowned out as the hall explodes into noise. Whoops, congratulations, outright screams of delight. One bunch of people start chanting "Re-mi-ssion, Re-mi-ssion!" while another lot start on "Daniel, Daniel" again, as everyone hugs Daniel and pounds him far less gently on the back than last week.

After a few moments, Father Thomas dashes through the door. "What on earth—?"

"Remission!" The boy with the letter shoves it under his nose. "Look, *right here*. Remission!"

"What!" The priest snatches the paper, inspecting it closely, his face breaking into a beaming smile. He wraps Daniel in a big hug, picking him right up and swinging him around three-sixty degrees, almost taking out the smallest kid present. "Daniel, this is fantastic news," he says as he deposits Daniel on the floor again.

"Yep." Daniel's own smile shines with dazzling intensity. For all his enthusiasm for heaven, he seems genuinely delighted by the results. Kinda surprised. But happy.

What did Ignatius say to Polycarp when he heard that the persecution of his church in Antioch had died down? That the news left him *resting without anxiety in God—so long as, by means of my suffering, I may reach God at the last.*

Daniel will get there in the end. No need for him to rush off early and upset everyone, right? So he can be happy about this.

Katie hurries in, wide-eyed. "What's going on? Sounds like a riot..." She sees everyone gathered around Daniel and grins—he texted her already. "Oh. Right."

Eventually, the celebration dies down, the pizza is passed out, and we manage to start the film. The first shot of the heroine has my heart in my mouth. Her hair shines a glorious blond in the opening lighting and she reminds me so much of Katie. Even when it turns out that, in normal lighting, her hair is actually a rich reddish color, I want to leap into the screen and come to her defense, as the...

"Is that guy seriously supposed to be the *hero*?" I hiss to Daniel, my fury overwhelming me at the way the lead actor is treating the Katie-actress. "He's a *creep*!"

Daniel grins. "You can't judge him for behaving the way his society has taught him to behave."

"Yeah," murmurs Katie, on my other side, looking approving—but slightly amused—at my outburst. "The real test is when someone is shown another way to behave—do they do it?"

True.

The film continues. Peter and Paul both make appearances. Peter laments about how he betrayed Jesus: *With a curse for the weakness of my body in the face of death.*

The phrase lodges in my brain, joining all the irritating words of Ignatius that have taken up residence there.

Ah-hah, the hero shows signs of improvement... Nope. He's promptly backslid. Ugh, what does the heroine see in him? I'd never treat Katie that way—or any woman.

Soon, Nero is planning a horrible persecution against the Christians as he seeks to blame them for his own atrocity. "When I have finished with these

Christians," sneers Peter Ustinov in a brilliantly deranged performance, "history will not be sure that they ever *existed.*"

The Catholic youth group roars with laughter, booing and catcalling. One boy even chucks a bit of pizza crust, whacking Nero on the nose. Guess this is the perfect audience to watch this film with!

Things go from bad to worse for the characters, though. Well, the hero finally buckles his sandals and mans up and starts treating the heroine properly. Other than that...

"It's the lions!" The woman's scream goes right through me like an ice-cold blade. "The *lions!*"

Those poor imprisoned Christians could use some help from Ignatius. He would explain that to be fed to the lions was a great honor...but I can identify with the Christians in this film more easily than with him. They're scared. Really scared. Like I would be. The room is really quiet, now—no one is eating. Are they just going to die horribly, scared and helpless?

No! Peter comes. The Christians begin to *sing.* Suddenly, they're *all* Ignatius, embracing their deaths. Lions, pyres, crucifixion, bull fighting—the Christians sing regardless. Trusting God. Nero foams and rages in fury. Everyone exults in his frustration. I exult in it. He's doing evil, and good is beating him. In such a strange, peaceful way, but good is winning and it makes me warm inside.

The film finishes with an improbable Hollywood

ending for the main protagonists, but the youth group is much quieter than last week as the credits play. Some of the closing words haunt me: *O Lord, wither goest thou? How can we know the way?*

Yeah, how? That's what I want to know.

"Did they really sing?" I ask Daniel in a low voice.

"What, the ancient Christians? Heck, yeah. They were famous for being joyful in the arena. It's why the persecutions were always so counter-productive."

But it turns out Katie's fuming about something earlier in the film. "I just can't believe that Roman guy let his 'true love'" she speaks sarcastically, making quote marks, "kill herself along with him. That whole scene was a *travesty* of true love. If he really loved her he'd have wanted her to survive, to go on, to love again, to..."

"...make loads of babies," teases Francis.

"Ha ha. But, yeah, Titanic, whatever its other faults as a love story, really got *that* right at the end."

Huh, I thought the scene was romantic. But I see what they mean, when they put it like that.

Daniel's nodding agreement with Katie. "Yeah, the fact that he acquiesced to her being his and his alone, forever, shows that deep down, he saw her as his property."

"Real love wants what's best for the other person!" Katie says, her eyes burning. "It sets free and liberates, it doesn't control and dominate! Real love is about freedom. Real love is…"

Daniel catches my eye and we both interrupt, "…holding a basin of puke!" We crack up. Katie glares at us, clearly feeling we're not taking her seriously, but after a moment she laughs too. It's impossible to be down today, not after Daniel's letter!

I yank my eyes from Katie's glowing face with severe difficulty.

Man, she is so pretty.

CHAPTER 12

Daniel's positively bouncing as we walk along the dark streets, heading for my house. My parents are allowing the two of us to view the hovercraft for a few minutes tonight, then Daniel's mum will collect him from my house. And my dad will lock the garage again until after our exams are over. Alas. But it's only a matter of weeks, now.

That letter, and my good news, and a great film have put Daniel in a pretty radiant mood. 'Cause, yeah, it *was* a good film, despite being old and pretty depressing at times...

"Shame there's no film next week," I remark.

"Yeah. But it's so close to exams, too many parents won't let people come. We're gonna watch Gladiator for our post-exam party. That's when we vote on what to watch in September. At the moment it's a tie between anime and—get this—horse films."

I grin. "Katie would like that."

"Yeah, it's getting the female vote, alright. I s'pose

some of them might be okay."

I picture the ratio of girls to boys in the youth group. Slightly more girls?

"We may just find out."

Daniel shoots me a look. Then grins even wider.

Huh? Oh, right. I've just made it clear I plan to keep attending.

He's in such a good mood, I feel I can finally say, "So, uh, you gonna go to the rescue center sometime and find a cat that needs a good home?"

He stops skipping and walks beside me more seriously. "I dunno. I'd really like to. But...is this a great time to get one? What about when I...uh, if I...oh, you know, university or...whatever. Do I just dump the cat on my parents? You know my mum's slightly allergic."

"But it'll get a good home for two years."

"Yeah. I wonder if I should get a really old one. But that's a bit unfair on Mum and Dad for the vet's bills. And on Clare for...y'know. She took it really hard. Maybe I should just—" He breaks off, stopping dead, eyes on the street ahead.

Three guys in balaclavas stand in front of us, but the balaclava doesn't stop me from recognizing the middle one. I grab Daniel's shoulder, pulling him with me as I step backwards. He's regained a lot of his energy, but how fast can he run?

A sound from behind me, and I shoot a quick glance that way. No, no, no, the rest of the Sick Kitties— sorry, Lions of *Allah*—are behind us. Nowhere to run.

"On our way back from church, are we, Razim?" sneers Sayeed. "In company with a notorious infidel?"

"It's a free country." My voice comes out tight, but doesn't quite shake.

"Not for your brothers in the faith, it isn't. Yet you keep company with the enemy!"

"You sound like a B-movie."

"Very funny. I could just let you burn. But it's too embarrassing to risk my....my *neighbor* turning apostate. And then I'd have to kill you."

Neighbor? Does he seriously think Daniel won't recognize him? What an ass.

An ass wearing a mask, with six guys at his back, probably all carrying knives. Oh man. At least Daniel is keeping quiet so far and letting me do the talking. I wouldn't put it past him to be a wise mouth if he doesn't realize how dangerous the new Sayeed might be.

"*Abbu* and *Ammi* have no problem with me attending Daniel's youth group. So let us pass."

"Oh yeah, you've got them wrapped around your little finger. *Just a youth group.* Well, if it's just a youth group, how do you explain these?" He holds up two small cards.

My stomach clenches. I don't quite keep my voice steady this time. "Uh...see the Arabic. Daniel wanted me to translate them. That's all." I try for some anger. "*And why the heck were you in my room?*"

Very deliberately, Sayeed rips each card in two and

tosses the pieces to the ground. "Nice try, Razim. As though he wouldn't just use an app."

Why *didn't* Daniel just use an app? Maybe he didn't think of it—or maybe he realized the card might interest me.

Well, he got that right. And now look where we are...

"Let's hear the *Shahada* from you," barks Sayeed. "Right now."

The Muslim declaration of faith. Say it just once, and you're supposedly a Muslim forever—according to people like Sayeed. I *have* said it before. But I don't want to say it again. I don't *believe* it. I'm so fed up with Sayeed trying to make me live a lie.

"I—" I break off. Because, on the other hand—seven guys with knives, and even if we could get past them, I doubt Daniel could outrun them for long.

But I really don't want to say it.

I hear the smirk in Sayeed's voice as he speaks again. "Not *you*. You're Muslim already. Let's hear the skinny infidel say it—then the problem is solved. He won't be an infidel anymore."

My heart accelerates, pounding even harder in my chest. Oh no. They're going after *Daniel*. My eyes dart around, looking for a gap in their ranks we could make a break through. Nothing. I edge Daniel backwards against the wall, trying to keep in front of him. He still doesn't speak, so I guess he has picked up how serious this is.

Sayeed recites the words of the Shahada, very

slowly and clearly, as though speaking to a toddler. "Your turn, skinny white boy."

Daniel stays quiet.

"*Say it!*"

I shoot Daniel a glance. He stands motionless, eyes fixed to Sayeed's balaclava, his face tense.

Sayeed recites the words again. "Speak, creamy!"

Finally, Daniel does speak, very firmly. "*There shall be no compulsion in religion.* I might be paraphrasing slightly, but that's from the Quran. I'm a Christian. Trying to force me to become Muslim is a sin in both our faiths."

Oh heck. Does he think my brother can be *reasoned* with?

"Get him!" At Sayeed's words, they all lunge forward. I try to block them, but a few seconds later, two of them are holding onto me and two have forced Daniel to his knees, twisting his arms behind him.

"Get off him!" I shout. Belatedly, I realize that, although we're alongside a derelict building right here, we're not that far from houses. If we can get someone to look out of their window... I draw a big breath. "*HELP*—" But my full volume yell chokes off as a big hand closes over my mouth. I try to bite, but a moment later one of the other guys is stuffing a rolled up t-shirt between my teeth like a horse's bit and yanking it tight behind my head.

"*Elp...Gerroff!*" Nope, no one's gonna hear me now! I try to kick, but my arm is twisted behind my back, making me gasp in pain and stand on tiptoe.

Sayeed stops in front of Daniel, pulling a knife from his pocket and unfolding it. *Uh-oh...*

"Last chance, milksop. Recite after me..."

Daniel stares up at him, his mouth firmly closed. I recognize the stubborn set of his jaw.

No, no, no... With this gag in my mouth I can't even tell him to say it, that it means nothing if he's forced, that Sayeed really might hurt him...

Scream for help, Daniel...something!

But after that film we just watched, he's probably more likely to sing a hymn, isn't he? *Fine, sing. LOUDLY!*

He just stays silent. I can see his shoulders moving slightly in the illumination from the street light, as he breathes quick and shallow.

Okay, so he is scared. He is taking this seriously. But he's still not gonna say it, is he?

"Teach him a lesson!" orders Sayeed.

The guys holding Daniel shove him to the ground and start kicking him.

"*Ge-off-im!*" I wrench as hard as I can, trying to get free, but the guy holding my arm behind my back yanks it up so high that tears of pain start in the corners of my eyes.

Daniel curls into a ball, trying to protect himself, grunting in agony as their feet slam into his chest, into his stomach...

"Enough."

90

They yank Daniel up into a kneeling position again. He's panting, his face screwed up with pain, blood flowing from a cut on his cheek.

"Right! Give him to me!" Sayeed grabs Daniel, shoves his fingers into his nostrils for grip and yanks his head back. Daniel's throat looks very long and pale in the sodium light as Sayeed sets the blade of the knife to his skin.

"*Say it.* Or I'll have your head off like a dandelion and solve the problem that way."

I can't see Daniel's face properly, but his chest shudders slightly as he draws in shaky breaths.

"*Ee-im-a-lone!*" I grunt around the gag.

Sayeed presses the knife harder. A drop of red runs down Daniel's neck. "Last chance. Say it."

But when I am close to the sword I am close to God; when I am among the wild beasts I am in company with God; provided only that I be so in the name of Christ Jesus... Ignatius' letter to the Smyrnaeans pops into my head.

Daniel opens his mouth at last and... Oh heck. He does sing. His voice is firm now. Ridiculously firm. He's mastered his fear.

"*O saving Victim, opening wide, the gate of heaven to us below, our foes press on from every side; Thine aid supply, Thy strength bestow...*"

Sayeed stiffens in rage. Deciding. Deciding what to do...

Ignatius, Jesus, anyone, help us!

More of Ignatius's words slip into my mind: *Suffer me to obtain pure light: only then shall I indeed be a man.*

Light.

Light!

My eyes dart around. Cars are parked all along the side of the road, the closest only feet away. A new BMW... The schematic unfolds in my mind, wiring, sensors, suspension... Yes!

They're concentrating so hard on keeping my *gag* in... *Hah! Thanks, Ignatius.* I throw myself forward, driving one foot with all the force I can muster into the best spot on the side of the car, succeeding in rocking it...hard enough? A second later, sound and light shatter the night as the car alarm goes off. Everyone with their hands free throws them up to shield their eyes from the dazzling LEDs.

"*Quick!*" Sayeed shoves Daniel away. "*Let's go!*"

The gag is wrenched from my mouth, spinning me around and almost taking my teeth with it as they sprint away. I stagger, falling against the car. By the time I straighten, they're gone. I dash over to Daniel as he slumps down on the paving slabs.

"Daniel? Daniel?" I wipe frantically at his neck with my hand, trying to clear the blood away, trying to see... "Daniel?"

I think...I think it's just a surface cut...

"I'm okay," he whispers. Voice tight with pain. *Is* he okay? His throat's not slit, but they roughed him up so badly...

I snatch out my phone and swipe it on. But I can already hear a siren, in the distance. Coming here? Did someone already see?

Daniel uncurls one arm from around himself, gripping my arm tightly. "Raz... Raz, promise me..."

"What?"

"Your brother...don't tell them it was him. I forgive him. You understand?"

"He doesn't deserve it!"

"Promise!"

He's lying there all pale and bloodied, his eyes burning into me with such intensity...the words just slip from my mouth... "Alright, I promise." *Ugh, I shouldn't have said that. What if Sayeed attacks someone else?*

But Daniel relaxes, easing his grip on my arm.

"*Daniel...*" I protest.

"Think of your parents," he whispers. He's shaking so hard. Shock? I'm only wearing a light cotton jacket, but I shrug it off and lay it over him, then stroke my phone on again and dial the emergency services. It's ringing. Good...

But the siren is almost here. Red and blue lights spill over us as a vehicle pulls up in the roadway.

I never thought I'd be so glad to see the police!

CHAPTER 13

I sit in the back of the squad car. I can't stop shaking. They searched me, took a description of the attackers— *seven guys, bigger than us, wearing dark clothes and balaclavas, slight London-Pakistani accent*—then let me wait with Daniel until the ambulance arrived. Wanted me to keep him awake and talking.

He just wanted someone to call his mum so she wouldn't worry. His skin looked such a sickly gray color as they lifted him into the ambulance on a stretcher, wrapped in one of those silver blankets. How bad is he hurt?

Will they catch Sayeed? I kept that stupid promise to Daniel and didn't name him, although the more I think about it, the more I'm certain that Daniel was wrong to ask it of me. Sayeed threatened me as well as Daniel, and I have to share a house with him. I mean, I don't think he's actually going to hurt me. I mean, not *hurt me, hurt me*. At least, not unless I do something totally crazy like become an apostate, which I'm not planning on. But what about any other Muslim in the area who decides to change religion? What about the next Christian like Daniel who Sayeed decides to attack?

Daniel said Christians are allowed self-defense, right? And, like, public defense? Surely that has to mean Sayeed belongs behind bars, for everyone's sake?

But I did promise…

Stupid, Razim, stupid!

I'm waiting, now, for them to take me to the police station to give a statement. Because I'm a witness. And a victim too, apparently, 'cause the gang twisted my arm and threatened me.

I can't stop shaking.

The front doors open and two of the officers settle into the seats. The two white ones who arrived first. "Okay, sorry about the wait," says the one who seems to be in charge. "We're heading to the station now."

The other one starts the engine, and we pull away.

I can't believe I'm sitting in the back of a police car. I'm not Sayeed. It's humiliating. Even though I'm not, technically, in trouble. It's scary, too.

I held my hands out, making sure they were visible when the officers got out of the car, the way *Abbu* taught me. This isn't the kind of area of the city where they were *likely* to be armed—but it is Saturday night and they were probably responding to a call about gang violence—so I did it anyway.

No guns, though. Just regular officers.

Maybe they'll send armed officers after Sayeed, maybe there'll be an accident...I wish.

I s'pose I shouldn't think like that. He is my brother. *Think of your parents*, Daniel said. But heck, I am so mad at Sayeed, right now.

I hunch in my seat as we drive along, though the glass is tinted and no one can see me. Fear drives my heart far too fast, annoying me with its cowardly pounding.

He will free you from every chain that binds you, Ignatius assured the Philadelphians. And, *I cling to the Gospel for refuge as to the incarnate Jesus.*

Daniel didn't stay afraid for long, even with a knife to his throat. But I just feel so totally helpless. Only Daniel knows where I am. And he's probably unconscious by now.

Shooting a look at the officers—they're not paying any attention—I slide my phone out of my pocket and text my parents.

Daniel was attacked – taken to hospital. Police taking me to the station to make statement.

I hit send. Only a moment later a reply comes from my mum, always the first to see a message: *I'll meet you there. Are you okay?!*

I'm not hurt, I send back.

After we've driven for a bit longer, staticky voices

speaking now and then from the radio and the policemen exchanging a few boring remarks about the evening's traffic, the boss officer twists slightly to look at me. "Oh, is there someone who can come and meet you at the station?"

"My mum's on her way."

"Ah, you're way ahead of us." They both laugh, then he just says, "Good," and faces forward again.

Their easy humor reassures me. I'm not Ignatius, on my way to my doom in chains.

Even if I feel like it.

+

When we arrive, they sit me in a private room out of the Saturday night chaos—because I'm a minor?— and let a medical officer loose on me. He prescribes hot chocolate and biscuits and a coat from lost property— I'm *still* shaking—and sits with me as we wait for *Ammi* to arrive. They want her present when they speak to me.

He encourages me to sip and eat, but doesn't force me to chat. I pull my phone out and open Ignatius's letters at random, seeking distraction. Philadelphians.

For my spirit ... knows both its origin and its destination.

My throat tightens. That's why Daniel is so calm, isn't it? He knows exactly where he's going. Further on in the letter, Ignatius says, *the Gospel is the perfection of immortality.*

Immortality again. Why is everything in my life about death, now? Blame Daniel. Except it's not his fault, is it?

Movement in the doorway...it's *Ammi*! I jump to my feet as she rushes towards me. I didn't want to cry in front of the police, but somehow I'm in her arms...

"They hurt Daniel..." Ugh, my face is pressed into her shoulder, words spurting out in between sobs. "I thought they were going to *kill* him... I couldn't stop them... I couldn't stop them, *Ammi*! They hurt him so badly..."

+

Ammi is very quiet as she drives me home. Is she angry? When they were doing all the routine questions and asked my religion, I just said, "Uh, culturally Muslim, I s'pose."

The woman's finger hovered over the keys: "Muslim, then?"

And I said, "No, put *No Religion*, then."

I said it a bit fiercely, in fact.

And *Ammi* gave me such a funny look. Kinda startled and...I don't know. And she's been so quiet since. Is she mad at me? Why? I mean, *she's* only culturally Muslim, right?

Somehow I got through the interview without breaking my promise to Daniel—or outright lying to the police. I kept hoping they'd ask me something I couldn't wriggle around, so I'd have a cast iron excuse to give Daniel—but they never quite did.

"Why did they only beat Daniel?"

"He's Christian, I'm not."

"So it was religiously motivated?"

"From what they were shouting at us, yeah."

"So they obviously knew who you both were?"

"Yeah, I think so."

"But you don't know who they were?"

"They were very careful about that."

"You didn't recognize any of them?"

"They were wearing full-face balaclavas!"

"Any guesses? Anyone been bullying either of you?"

"I...really couldn't name anyone. I mean...it could've been *anyone*. I can't single someone out like that."

"So a lot of people object to you being friends with Daniel?"

"I wouldn't say that. But he doesn't exactly hide his faith."

It seemed to go on forever. But finally they thanked me, a photographer took photos of the hand marks on my upper arms, and the marks from the gag around my mouth, and we were free to go.

Whether they actually *believe* I don't know who it was... Well, I can't be the first gang victim who isn't prepared to squeal. Maybe I can get Daniel to change his mind. I mean, Sayeed would go to prison for this, right? Just imagine, not having him in the house anymore! It would be bliss. I'd be free to...to do whatever I wanted.

Think of your parents.

I glance at *Ammi*'s troubled face as we walk to the

front door. They were so humiliated when Sayeed got in trouble all those times before. If he was actually sent to *prison*...and for attacking *Daniel*. They've been friends with the Whelkes for *years*.

Why is nothing *simple* anymore?

"Razim, are you alright?" *Abbu* is waiting in the hall. He was probably round at his darts club when the text arrived.

"Yeah, I'm fine. Do you know how Daniel is?"

"His mum called a few minutes ago. He's had some scans, and he's stable. The doctors don't need to do anything more tonight, and he's asleep, so that sounds positive."

I let out a long, shaky breath, my throat tightening again. But it's not hard to hold the tears in this time, because I can see Sayeed's foot at the top of the stairs. My jaw clenches, everything clenches. Heck, I'm angry.

"I'm, uh, I'm going to bed."

"Yes... *Alhamdulillah*, it's one-thirty in the morning," says Ammi. "Yes, you get to bed, *beta*. Get some sleep. I'll bring your *Abbu* up to date."

I catch snatches of their soft voices as I head up the stairs and they move into the lounge.

"...religiously motivated..."

"...No, surely..."

"...because Daniel's Christian..."

"...people like that...in this area...!"

In this area? Closer than that, Abbu!

I reach the top of the stairs. Sayeed is still lurking on

the landing. In fact, he backs me up against my door the moment I arrive, his hand pressing my shoulder, grinding me back into my door frame. He knows lots of ways of hurting me quietly.

"*Did you squeal?*"

I eye him in disgust. "You don't think you'd have noticed by now, if I had, you moron?"

Despite the insult, he takes his hand away, his face relaxing in relief—and maybe some surprise. "Maybe you're not a total lost cause."

"Get this straight, Sayeed," I hiss, rage boiling inside me. "I didn't keep quiet because you're my brother. As far as I'm concerned, that's a cosmic accident that gets more unfortunate by the year. I didn't even keep quiet for *Ammi* and *Abbu*. I kept quiet because Daniel wanted me to. Because he forgives you. Crazy, if you ask me, but apparently that's what Christians do. So if you want someone to thank for the fact that you're not sitting in a cell right now—thank *Jesus Christ*."

His fist shoots out, but I'm expecting it and dodge. *Thud*. His knuckles hit my door instead.

"Boys?" *Abbu*'s voice calls from the lounge. "You're not fighting again, are you?"

"No, *Abbu*," lies Sayeed smoothly through gritted teeth, clutching his fist. "I just dropped something."

"Well, get to bed, both of you. I know you wanted to stay up because you were worried about Razim, but he's back now."

"Yes, *Abbu*."

But Sayeed immediately reaches for me again.

"Get your hands off!" I hiss. "I swear, you keep bothering me, and I'll tell the police the truth!"

"Yeah? And then you'll be up for lying to them."

"I'll tell them you threatened to kill me."

"Yeah?" While I'm watching his right fist, his left hand darts in and closes around my throat, squeezing hard enough to hurt. "You know what?" He puts his face very close. "You won't be lying."

CHAPTER 14

Daniel's running along the beach, laughing. I dash after him, my feet kicking up the sand.

"Daniel! Slow down!"

"Come on! It's going to be wonderful!"

"Daniel, stop! It might not be safe..."

"There's nothing to be afraid of, Raz." He grabs my wrist and pulls me after him, through a big, dark archway in the headland. "Come on!"

But it's not more beach we stumble out onto. It's an arena. Packed tiers of seating rise all around. The crowd greets our appearance with a savage roar. Panic clenches my guts.

"Daniel, we have to get out of here! Right now!"

Daniel just smiles at me. "Relax, Raz. Everything will be fine."

A coughing roar. I spin around. Lions are bounding out of a little gateway in the wall. One, two, three...heck, eight.

"You call that fine?"

Daniel just grins at me. He raises his arms high, to the

sky, *turning in a slow, ecstatic circle as he sings: "O saving Victim, opening wide, the gate of heaven to us below, our foes press on from every side; Thine aid supply, Thy strength bestow..."*

"Daniel!" Three lions grab his arm, his side, his leg, dragging him down. He doesn't struggle, though pain twists his face—but it doesn't touch the peace in his eyes.

"Daniel!" Teeth sink into my thigh, holding me back— even as I struggle to get free, one of the lions casually ducks its head and rips Daniel's throat out. Blood spatters across my face...

"No!" But now there are teeth around my *throat...so tight... I can't breathe...*

Not teeth. Sayeed's hands. Choking me. I'm in my bedroom. I was dreaming...I try to struggle, try to kick him, but my covers tangle around me and I just...can't...breathe...

I wake with a horrible jolt and lie, panting and shaking. After a moment, I roll over, my gaze flying to my door. The tension bar I designed and built to keep it closed after the toilet incident is still wedged firmly in place, preventing Sayeed from entering with anything short of a full rhinoceros impression.

Ow. My arms hurt. And my mouth... What...?

Memory comes back in a rush. My phone buzzes. I sit up, ignoring the soreness, and grab it. Two texts from Daniel.

Are you okay?

I'm fine.

Oh, sure you are. Guess he just woke up. Or just got hold of his phone. Sunlight blazes around the curtains. It's nine o'clock.

Visitors OK? I text.

Yes, comes the speedy reply.

I scramble out of bed, throw my clothes on and hurry downstairs. *Ammi*'s folding laundry in the utility room.

"*Ammi*, I'm going to the hospital to see Daniel."

"Not without some breakfast, you're not!"

I groan, but head for the kitchen. It'll be quicker than arguing.

Sayeed's sitting at the dining table. I ignore him, grabbing a plate and a bagel and a sharp knife. Before I can get the butter from the fridge, my phone rings. I grab it out, swiping 'answer.' Only as I raise it to my ear does it register that the caller ID was Daniel's mum, not Daniel. But instead of "Hi, Mrs. Whelkes" what comes out is: "Is Daniel okay?"

"Yes, yes, sorry, Razim. I'm not trying to scare you. Are *you* alright?"

"I'm fine. You sure Daniel is okay?" Of course, he was texting me only a few moments ago.

"Yes, it's Clare, actually. I just want to keep things normal for her this morning—I, uh, was afraid she'd think Daniel was really sick again if she knew he was in hospital, so I told her he was with you"—she sounds

105

guilty—"and Daniel's dad can't get back from his business trip until early afternoon. I just wondered if you could come and keep Daniel company at the hospital? Then, uh, I didn't even lie to Clare, really."

"Of course. I was just about to set off there anyway." Over at the table, Sayeed gives me an evil glare. I glare back.

"Oh, thank you, Engineer-Brain." That's always been her nickname for me. "You're sure you're alright?"

"Barely a scratch on me. I'm really sorry. The thugs just went for Daniel..."

"You don't need to apologize, Razim! The only silver lining is that they didn't hurt you too."

"How is Daniel?"

"Oh, well..." Her voice shakes a little. "They gave him a few scans last night. He has some lung contusions so they're giving him a little oxygen to help with that. Some broken ribs. And minor internal bleeding in the abdomen. They thought it should stop on its own by this morning, but they'll take him for another scan later, to check. If it hasn't stopped, they'll have to operate, but...well, he'll...he'll be alright, either way. Don't you worry."

I'm shaking. Shaking with fury as I stare at my brother. My fists clench so tight on what they're holding that it hurts. *Lung contusions...oxygen...internal bleeding... operate...* Heck, Daniel wouldn't hurt a fly and they... they... Even my thoughts sputter with rage. I still have the sharp knife in my fist. Part of me wants to...to...

Sayeed abruptly gets up and leaves the room.

"Razim? Are you still there?"

The red haze eases its grip a little. Slowly, deliberately, I put the knife down. A bully. A bully and a coward. That's what Sayeed is.

I return the phone to my ear. "Uh, yes, Mrs. Whelkes. It sounds bad but I'm...I'm glad it isn't any worse."

"So are we, Razim. So are we." But her voice still trembles.

When she hangs up, I grab the unbuttered bagel and go into the hall. "I'm off now, *Ammi*."

"I'll drop you off, *beta*, it's the least I can do. Poor Daniel. I have some errands to run, anyway." She turns and picks up her car keys, reaching for her handbag, then hesitates. "Oh, do you want to see the hovercraft first? Your *abbu* said you could..."

I head for the front door. "Not now *Ammi*. Please can we just go?"

+

"So, then I realized I'd told the policeman all about how I kicked a *brand new* BMW as hard as I could. And I'm looking at him and going, *uh-oh*. But he didn't react, so I had to ask, 'Er, am I going to be in trouble?' And he just laughed and said 'No, you're not in trouble. That was very quick thinking on your part. You may just have—'" I break off. *...saved your friend's life*, is what the interviewer said, but I'm embarrassed to repeat it.

"May just have saved my life?" Daniel grins at me.

"They told Mum all about it last night, when they were filling her in a bit better on what happened to me. I didn't really see what you did—I was too busy offering my soul to God right then. Thanks, man. You're the hero of the hour."

His face is bruised, sutures holding that cut closed, a little oxygen pipe runs under his nostrils, and he's got an IV drip in each arm, but he's chirpy cheerful. The head end of the bed is raised so that he's almost sitting up properly.

Hero? I shake my head. "No, I'm not. It's my fault this happened..."

"It's not *your* fault. Don't be stupid."

"I shouldn't have taken those cards home. I knew what Sayeed is like."

"Razim, you said it last night, it's a free country. If you want to"—he makes an expansive gesture—"to paper your room in prayer cards, you're allowed."

A ridiculously large sigh escapes from me. "It's not that simple."

"Okay, maybe not, but...stop blaming yourself. Blame where it's due. We both know where."

"Yeah, about that..."

"No."

"Let me out of my promise! I—"

"*No.*"

"Why are you protecting him? He doesn't deserve it!"

"You don't forgive someone because they *deserve*

108

it."

"Why else!"

"Because God forgives *us*, and *we* don't deserve it!"

"Then why does *He* do it?"

"Because he loves us, Raz!"

Love. We're back to love again. What did Ignatius say in Smyrnaeans, the one letter I haven't finished reading yet? *For I have seen that you are perfected in an immovable faith, as if you were nailed body and soul to the cross of our Lord Jesus Christ, and rooted in love through His blood.*

I *have* seen. Literally seen with my own eyes. Yesterday. Daniel wouldn't yield. Does his mum know? Does it terrify her the way it terrifies me?

I open my mouth again...

"Stop, Raz. You know he'd go to prison for this! You think that would help him? People get radicalized in prison."

"Er, did you miss the memo? It's a bit late to worry about that!"

"You know what I mean; people network in there and stuff. At the moment he's just a petty thug, and he's still got a chance to turn his life around. The moment we hand him in, that chance is *gone*. All that's left is…is anger and…and hating everyone and everything!" Daniel's eyes are growing wild. "He'll end up doing something really big and bad or he'll be in prison for the rest of his life, or both! God gives us every chance He possibly can to change for the better—well, I want to do the same for him!"

"You think Sayeed's gonna *stop*? Just because you forgave him? He doesn't care about that. You defied him. I bet he hates you now as much as he hates me. You should put him away, then we'll both be safe! And what about the next person he goes after? Don't you care about that?"

"No!" He sounds even more frenzied. "So many saints have forgiven their attackers and even protected them! It's the right thing to do!"

"How about you ask your Father Thomas about that if you're so sure? And we'll do what *he* says?"

Daniel's cheeks flush red as he jabs a finger towards himself for emphasis. "*I'm* the one who'll be standing before God, explaining why the one time in my life something really serious was actually done to me, I failed to turn the other cheek, failed to truly love! Me, not you, not Father Thomas! Me! Unless I literally cannot find a way to evade the question without lying, I'm not telling!" He grabs his Bible from the bedside table, flips it open to a bookmark and thrusts it towards me, pointing at the page. "Read, Raz! Then maybe you'll understand."

I recoil, a wild sense of panic exploding inside me. I can't read that!

"No."

"Well, if you want the answer, Raz, it's in here." He places the book down on top of the bedcovers, within easy reach of me.

I stare at it. I want to stretch out and take it. Read. Find out... No. I can't. That's not like reading Ignatius's letters, that's... It's different. Somehow.

I might as well be standing on a cliff, about to jump into a wild, foaming sea. The moment I step off, that's it. The point of no return... Why do I feel like reading that book would be like that? Stupid. It's just words. Yet...

I can't.

I don't *dare*.

I refuse to.

With a huge effort, I wrench my eyes from the fatal book, groping for an unrelated remark. But I've been silent too long. Daniel's uninjured cheek rests against the pillow, his eyes are closed, his breathing deep and even. Sleeping.

Unstoppably, my gaze is drawn back to the Bible.

If you want the answer...

Why does Daniel love Sayeed this much? Even when I know he doesn't even *like* Sayeed. Even though I think he may be wrong about how he's expressing that love. I mean, can leaving Sayeed free to carry on doing stuff like this really be loving him? It can't be good for Sayeed either, right? All the same, the intensity of Daniel's love stuns me, confuses me. It's like I've been walking around with him for the better part of two years, and I've never realized how deep it really goes. How is he like that?

Do I want the answer? Yes.

Only in the name of Christ Jesus, for the sake of sharing

his sufferings, could I face all these things, said Ignatius to the Smyrnaeans, *for He who became a perfect man inwardly strengthens me.*

But how? How has Daniel faced all this? *How, how, how...* Why can't I understand?

I pick up the book. It's surprisingly heavy, the wafer-thin paper making a dense wad. I lay it on my lap.

Put it back, Razim. It's not worth it.

Isn't it? I see Daniel spinning in that joyful circle in my dream; hear him singing on his knees last night as he waited to die...

How can it not be worth it?

I bend my neck and look. Daniel pointed roughly... there. That's...what they call the Lord's Prayer, right?

My eye skates over the semi-familiar words, and I read on:

"14 If you forgive others their transgressions, your heavenly Father will forgive you. 15 But if you do not forgive others, neither will your Father forgive your transgressions."

Okay, I see why Daniel thinks he needs to do what he's doing. But surely it has to be okay to turn Sayeed in, regardless? I mean, Christian countries have always had legal systems and judges and prisons, right? Daniel talked about saints, but surely the norm has to be justice and...and protecting people?

Well, I won't change his mind while he's this worked up about it. He was in a real state. Maybe when he calms down he'll listen to reason.

My eyes return to the book on my lap. So…what about love? And faith? And…gentleness?

I flick on at random, and find myself at the beginning of a book called Mark. I can't stop myself, now.

I read.

CHAPTER 15

Words lodge themselves in my brain as I turn the flimsy pages.

> "Whoever wishes to come after me must deny himself, take up his cross, and follow me. [25] For whoever wishes to save his life will lose it, but whoever loses his life for my sake will find it."

Whoever wishes to save his life will lose it? Okay, that's... scary. Why am I reading this? Surely after last night I should just close this book and walk away? But...longing rips through me, building like a dam filled almost to breaking point.

> "[26] What profit would there be for one to gain the whole world and forfeit his life?"

That reminds me of that moment with the hover-craft, when I realized that the one thing, the object, that I had been craving for over a year meant absolutely nothing to me compared to having Daniel well.

I'm a sputtering bulb, barely attached to a circuit through a poor connection, like I'm *this close* to under-standing...what?

"Which commandment is the first of all?" a young man asks Jesus. And Jesus answers:

[29] *Jesus replied, "The first is this: 'Hear, O Israel! The Lord our God is Lord alone!* [30] *You shall love the Lord your God with all your heart, with all your soul, with all your mind, and with all your strength.'* [31] *The second is this: 'You shall love your neighbor as yourself.' There is no other command-ment greater than these."*

Love.

Like placing the last drop of solder onto that dodgy circuit and closing it, two things click in my mind.

The fundamental thing about Islam is total submission to God, that's what Islam *means*. And that's a very good thing, at least, it is if you do it the way Noora does it—and involves a lot of love. But the fundamental thing about Christianity *is* love itself. Loving God. And that's even better.

Because that's the answer. Love is the answer. I keep asking *how*, wanting some engineering solution to my spiritual dilemmas, a nice wiring diagram to follow, hard proof, to make it all make sense. But love *is* the how. God loves us. And we should love him. And it's *because* we love him, that we should serve him. *Not* the other way around.

Let him who is able, receive this truth, whispers Ignatius.

I read and read, turning the pages as fast as I can, as Jesus allows himself to be arrested, not fighting back, as he dies, forgiving his killers, as he rises again and tells his disciples to go and proclaim the Gospel—love, right?—to all nations.

Ignatius has something to say about this, to:

> *But people who fail to preach Christ Jesus, they are in my judgment no more than tombstones and graves of the dead, upon which are written only the names of men. Flee therefore the wicked devices and snares of the prince of this world, lest you be conquered by his artifices and grow weak in your love. Rather be joined all together with an undivided heart.*

Tombs... Without Jesus we are simply dead—or not fully alive.

...Weak in love...be joined all together...

Some of the final words of Mark fill my mind: *Whoever believes and is baptized will be saved...*

"Raz? Are you okay?"

I look up, startled. My cheeks feel cold as I move my head. Oh. I'm crying. "I...uh..." I grip the Bible tightly. "I *want* this. I want it."

"Uh..." A flicker of dismay crosses Daniel's face, quickly replaced by a determined smile. "Yeah, have it. It's yours."

I laugh, though it comes out half a sob. "No, I'm not trying to take your *Bible*." He's been scribbling on and annotating that thing for eighteen leukemia-racked months. "I want..." Heck, I'm as articulate as a three-year-old. "Baptize me?"

His mouth drops open, but his eyes light up. "Yes!"

I put the Bible down and slide the glass of water closer to him, then drop to my knees beside the bed so he can reach me without moving.

"Are you...are you sure?" he asks, more hesitantly. "*Really* sure?"

"Yes!" My heart's pounding so hard it feels like fear and longing are having a fistfight inside my chest. "If I wait, if I let the fear start talking to me...I might chicken out. But I've never wanted anything as much as I want this! Please, Daniel, save me from...from *myself*, okay? Do it!"

"Okay! Here goes. Can you kinda, tilt your head back? That's good." That puts me in about the same position he was in last night when Sayeed threatened to cut his head off, but this is the opposite of murder so I hold still. I close my eyes as he tips the water over my forehead, three times, reciting as he does so, "Razim, I baptize you in the name of the Father, and of the Son, and of the Holy Spirit." He traces a cross on my wet forehead and grins at me, joy blazing from his face. "It's done. Razim, we are now actually brothers. In Christ!"

He reaches out as though inviting me in for a hug but I draw away, shaking my head. Broken ribs. Internal bleeding. Yeah, I'm not touching him.

"Ah." He thinks better of it and drops his arms again, but his smile stays on. "Raz, I could sing again! When did this happen?"

"Well, it...only made sense just now. But I think I've finally been considering it properly for a week or two. Deep down. Hadn't admitted it to myself."

"That's why you came to the youth group at last!"

"Yeah, I think it probably is."

Daniel actually hums a few bars to himself, one of his Christian pop songs, still grinning like mad.

I can't stop grinning either. I feel so light, like I've shed all the doubts and confusion and turmoil that's dogged me since he got ill. I'm a Christian. I am a Christian.

I've made my choice. I'm pretty sure I'm gonna feel very, very scared, soon enough, but right now I'm just going to enjoy the euphoria. I can't wait to tell Katie!

There's a tap on the door. "Hi, Daniel." It's Father Thomas, peering in. "Oh, hi, Razim."

Daniel glances around as though looking for a clock, seeming taken aback. "It's Sunday, right? How long did I sleep for? Are the morning Masses finished?"

"You slept for ages," I tell him. "I read the book of Mark, and dipped into John."

"Wow. Even at your reading speed, that was a good nap."

"It's after one o'clock," says the priest. "Your mum told me what happened, so I've brought you the Blessed Sacrament."

Jesus… He's got the physical Jesus with him, like at Mass.

"Wonderful!" says Daniel, beaming again. "Can Razim receive too or does he have to get confirmed first?" Confusion covers the priest's face so he adds, "I've just baptized him! Isn't it fantastic?"

Father Thomas stares at Daniel for a moment, then at me. My grin wilts into a nervous smile, because something about the priest's gob-smacked expression tells me that he doesn't find this fantastic at all. Daniel's lost his smile too.

"You really baptized him?" Father Thomas finally asks Daniel.

"Er...yep. I did it right, I promise."

"I bet you did." Father Thomas sinks down in a chair and puts his head in his hands with a groan, like he's developed an instant headache.

"Uh...it *is* fantastic, isn't it?" says Daniel weakly.

Father Thomas rubs his temples for a moment, then finally raises his head.

"From a spiritual point of view, it's fantastic for Razim, yes." He looks at me. "Razim, congratulations and welcome. I apologize for greeting what is essentially happy news with such a lack of enthusiasm. But

119

Daniel has just dropped a big mess in my lap." He eyes Daniel, who now stares, his eyes wide with dismay. "Inadvertently, I suspect. Though I'm surprised you didn't know better, Daniel."

Daniel's brows draw together suddenly, and he bites his lip. "Oh... Why didn't I think? Lay people are only supposed to baptize in an emergency."

"It was an emergency!" I say. "My soul needed saving!"

"Not that kind of emergency. You needed to be bleeding to death at my feet or something like that." Daniel's gaze shifts back to Father Thomas. "I don't know how I forgot... I do *know* all about that..." The confusion in his eyes is tipping into distress.

Father Ben reaches out and touches one of the IV lines in Daniel's wrist, tracing it for a moment, then nodding. "You're on morphine. Designed to ease pain, not promote good decision making."

Morphine? Heck, no wonder he's so cheerful! That must be because of the broken ribs. And maybe the internal injuries.

"But, Father," Daniel says, "it's really not *that* big a deal, right? That I did it instead of you?"

"If it was just that, it wouldn't be. But Razim, you're, what, sixteen, same as Daniel?"

I nod.

"So, Razim's a minor. It's against canon law to baptize him without his parents' permission, unless he's in danger of death."

"Really?" Daniel's eyes go even wider. Clearly this is something he didn't know. "Why?"

"In a nutshell, the supernatural law of the New Covenant does not cancel out the natural authority of parents over their children. Oh, the baptism's valid, right and tight. But it makes an awkward situation. Razim, do you think you can gain retroactive permission from your parents?"

My stomach drops. "P-Permission?" A couple of weeks ago I'd have assumed they wouldn't really be that bothered. But now I'm not so sure. The way *Ammi* reacted to me not wanting to be labeled as Muslim... How worried they were about whether the youth group was religious... I've a nasty feeling that having a son who doesn't really practice would be a very different thing than having a son who's actually apostate. "Isn't it...isn't it a bit late for that?"

"Yes, I suppose it is. And from your expression, the permission wouldn't be forthcoming, anyway." He glances at Daniel, who's looking seriously deflated. "If you'd come to me, one of the things I'd have made very sure about was that Razim understood that for someone of his cultural background, conversion can have a very serious impact on his life."

I snort softly. "Yeah? After last night, you think we're not both up to speed about that?"

"Huh. Maybe you are. Well, it's too late for you to wait until you're eighteen and free to make your own decisions with fewer consequences."

"And what if he was hit by a bus while waiting to be eighteen?" mutters Daniel. "It's not like anything fatal *ever* happens to teenagers."

Father Thomas fixes him with a stern look. "You know all about Baptism of Desire, Daniel. And he could still have made a personal commitment and prayed and come to church."

Daniel hangs his head again, but his gaze darts to mine for a moment and I know he's thinking maybe I got lucky that he didn't know all this. I'm kinda thinking the same.

The priest's lip twists as though he also knows Daniel well enough to read his mind on this one. But when Daniel carries on avoiding his eyes, he sighs. "I'm not *angry* with you, Daniel. You were trying to do the right thing, and I think we can assign the blame to the morphine. What's done is done. Razim, you will need religious instruction so you can be confirmed and receive Holy Communion. I will try and sort out a baptismal certificate. As for telling your family — I will leave it up to you when and how to do so."

He hesitates. "Just...please be careful."

Be careful.

Now the fear hits, like a bath of freezing water.

I am a Christian.

I am an *apostate*.

CHAPTER 16

"Well, go on," says Noora, smiling from the screen. "What's this big secret you want to tell me?"

I've decided to practice on Noora, the sweetest, gentlest, kindest of my relatives. Maybe once I've told her, she can help me figure out the best way to tell *Ammi* and *Abbu*.

"Um..."

"Oh, come on, Raz. You can tell me anything. Have you started praying again, tell me that's it!"

Praying, yeah, a lot, but not the way she wants for me.

"I, uh..." I stare at her image on the screen. "I..." She definitely doesn't think apostates should *die*. She's told me lots of reasons why not. But how will she react? Sadness, definitely. Understanding? Anger? Rejection?

"I..."

"What, Raz?"

"I...I really like Katie."

Noora bursts out laughing. "*That's* your big secret,

coz? Well, it's no secret to *me*. I thought you were about to tell me something *serious*!"

I shrug weakly. "Well, it's...serious for me."

Her face sobers. "Yeah, I suppose Sayeed will give you a hard time if you date a Christian. Well, it is acceptable, and he ought to know that, but...I'd think carefully about it, if I were you. Even if you do really like her. I know how you feel right now, I know you say you've no intention of practicing again, but your faith is your faith. Big differences of religion make for difficult marriages. So unless you think she's likely to convert..."

I snort. "Katie? Not likely."

"Then don't rush into anything, is my advice. *Inshallah*, what am I saying, you're only sixteen, anyway." She laughs, then turns her head, listening. "Oh, I have to go. They're starting the call to prayer. Take care of yourself, coz."

"Bye, Noora."

Her image winks out, and I stare numbly at the screen. If I can't even bring myself to tell Noora...how will I ever tell *Ammi* and *Abbu*?

The fear nips at me again, but I turn my thoughts determinedly to the words of Saint Ignatius of Antioch that I've memorized as a prayer:

Lord, let me please You under whom I fight,
and from whom I receive my wages.
Let me never be found a deserter.
Let my baptism be my shield;

my faith my helmet;
my love my spear;
my patience my full armor.
Let me lay up my good deeds
as a soldier deposits his savings,
that I may one day receive what is due to me.
May I be patient and gentle with all,
as God is towards me.
Amen.

Patient and gentle with all...

Yeah, you know what the worst thing is about being a Christian?

I had to forgive Sayeed.

Yeah, I should have seen that one coming!

But actually, it felt really good. *Radical* love.

Although: I asked Father Thomas about the whole Sayeed – police thing. Hypothetically, y'know, without naming names—though he probably saw through that—and he said that while Daniel is correct that some saints have done just what Daniel's doing, sometimes with stunning spiritual results, as a general rule someone like that ought to be handed over to the authorities "for the safety of society." So, actually, I was right. Daniel's still being super stubborn, though, even now he isn't on morphine.

On the plus side, Sayeed seems to understand what a near miss he's had, and he's actually backed off a bit. Mostly he just glowers, now.

If he knew I was a Christian, though... My heart thuds uncomfortably.

But the icon of Saint Ignatius flashes into my mind; his calm gaze spearing my soul.

I breathe out slowly, feeling steadier. Because one thing is certain.

He who gave Saint Ignatius the courage to face lions will surely give me the courage to do the same.

You can make a difference!

Reviews and recommendations are vital to any author's success. If you liked this book, please write a short review—a few lines are enough—and tell your friends about the book too.
You will help the author to create new stories and allow others to share your enjoyment.

Your support is important. Thank you.

DON'T MISS RAZIM'S OTHER STORY

Read a Sneak Peek on page 156!

DISCUSSION QUESTIONS

1) *Razim doesn't understand Daniel's faith, and the peace it brings him despite his illness.*
- Why do you think this is?
- Can you relate to Razim? In what way?
- Is there anything about Daniel's faith that you find attractive/interesting?

2) *Saint Ignatius of Antioch greets his death sentence with joy, and considers it an honor.*
- Why do you think he feels this way?
- Is there any suffering in your life that you accept with joy?
- Why is this so hard for us, as humans, to do?
- What makes it possible?
- Is this something you want?

3) *Sayeed considers that he and Razim are Muslims simply because their parents are. Razim believes that faith has to be a free choice. Similarly, the Catholic Church believes that although baptism leaves an indelible mark on the soul, which can never be removed, a Christian must choose every day of their life to love and serve God.*
- Which viewpoint makes most sense to you?
- Why?

4) *Christians living in earlier times (such as in Ancient Rome or Jesuit missionaries undertaking extremely dangerous missions in pagan lands) sometimes had a keen desire for martyrdom.*

- Does this differ from the way modern Christians see martyrdom today? In what ways?
- Do you feel you understand how earlier Christians viewed martyrdom?
- Does their attitude seem strange to you?
- Why/Why not?
- Thousands of Christians live under persecution today in many parts of the world. How do you think they could relate to the early martyrs?

5) *The Catholic Church sets out something called 'Just War Doctrine' which is the criteria by which Catholics 'with a responsibility for the common good' can discern whether involvement in an armed conflict is morally acceptable.*

- Have you heard of 'Just War Doctrine' (also known as 'Just War Theory') before?
- Are you familiar with the criteria? (You can find them in the Catholic Catechism, No. 2309)
- Think of a conflict that is going on in the world today (or a historical conflict) and spend a little time applying 'Just War Doctrine' to it. Would you personally consider it morally acceptable to participate in that conflict?

6) *Some Christians like St. Ignatius (and Daniel) choose not to fight back when personally threatened, and most priests, monks, nuns and religious brothers and sisters would consider it inappropriate to do violence. Different reasons for such a decision are mentioned by Daniel in the story.*
- Can you remember what they are?
- Do you agree with the different reasons?
- Why/Why not?

7) *There are also movements within the Church (as well as groups of Christians not in full communion) who adhere to total pacifism on a communal rather than a personal level.*
- Do you know what 'pacifism' is?
- Do you know of any Catholic movements or groups of other Christians that take this stance?
- Do you agree with them?
- Why/Why not?

8) *Daniel mentions several theories as to whether there might or might not be animals in heaven in some form or other.*
- Had you heard all these theories before?
- Do any of them make particular sense to you?
- Why/Why not?
- Did you understand why Daniel claimed that, ultimately, all such theories miss the point?

- Do you agree?
- Why/Why not?

9) *Saint Ignatius considered obedience to one's bishop to be very important because the bishop stands as Christ to his flock, and the hierarchical structure of the Church helps to safeguard objective truth.*
- Do you understand what is meant by 'objective truth'?
- Do you think that it is important?
- Why/Why not?

10) *Both St. Ignatius and Daniel find themselves in situations where they must either deny their faith or accept death.*
- If you found yourself in such a situation, what would you want to do?
- Do you think you would manage to do it?
- Why/Why not?
- How might you act from now on to increase your chances of being able to make the hard choice and stick to it, in the event that such a situation ever occurred?

THE LETTERS OF SAINT IGNATIUS

One of the most readable translations is found in:
- *Early Christian Writings: The Apostolic Fathers*
(Penguin Classics) Edited by Andrew Louth and
Maxwell Staniforth
This book also contains *The Epistle of Saint Polycarp*
and other contemporary documents.

Many other translations of the letters are available,
including Public Domain translations that can be
found free online (many of which I have made
reference to while preparing this book).

Most are conveniently listed here:
https://early.xpian.info/eng/ignatiusofantioch.html

Of the free translations listed at the link above,
two of the most readable are:
- Cyril C. Richardson (translated ~1953), *Early
Christian Fathers* (published 1953)

- Alexander Roberts/James Donaldson (translated
~1867), *Ante-Nicene Fathers* volume 1 (published 1885)

There is also a very literal translation that is closer to
reading the text in the original language.
- 2012 Literal Translation, Anonymous

**TO READ
ST. IGNATIUS'S LETTER TO THE ROMANS,
TURN TO PAGE 138.**

MORE INFORMATION

Bearing God: The Life and Works of St. Ignatius of Antioch the God-Bearer by Andrew Stephen Damick
A non-fiction biography by an Orthodox priest.

Saint Ignatius of Antioch - Benedict XVI's General Audience Address, March 14, 2007
Available free at:
https://www.vatican.va/content/benedict-xvi/en/audiences/2007/documents/hf_ben-xvi_aud_20070314.html

Learning Christ: Ignatius of Antioch & the Mystery of Redemption by Gregory Vall
A very thorough scholarly examination of Saint Ignatius's theology by a Catholic theologian.

PRAYER TO SAINT IGNATIUS OF ANTIOCH

St. Ignatius,
it was said you converted to Christianity as a child.

Along with St. Polycarp, you were said to be a
disciple of St. John the Evangelist. St. Peter himself
appointed you bishop of Antioch.

Because you called yourself Theophorus, or 'God
bearer', a tradition arose that you were one of the
children Christ Himself held and blessed
in the Gospels.

You took your duties as bishop seriously—protecting
your flock from heresy, being a gentle pastor, and
protecting your people from persecutions.

When you were asked to make a sacrifice to the gods
and refused, you were arrested and sent to Rome.

On the way you wrote several letters to the people of
Antioch.

Under Emperor Trajan, you were sent to the
colosseum to be devoured by lions.

You died as a brave soldier of Christ.

St. Ignatius, you are one of the Fathers of the Church;
pray for Her now as She gears up for Her final battle.

St. Ignatius, you were a kind and tender pastor; pray for all our parish priests, that they may draw people ever more closely to Christ by exemplifying His mercy and goodness.

St. Ignatius, you were not afraid to die as a martyr for our Lord; pray for all those who are dying this day. Amen.

St. Ignatius of Antioch, pray for us!

- + -

A PRAYER FOR THE DEAD

Traditionally attributed to Saint Ignatius of Antioch

Receive in tranquility and peace,
O Lord, the souls of your servants who have departed this present life to come to you.

Grant them rest and place them in the habitations of light, the abodes of blessed spirits.

Give them the life that will not age,
good things that will not pass away,
delights that have no end,
through Jesus Christ our Lord.

Amen.

SAINT IGNATIUS ANTIOCH NOVENA

Feast Day: 17th October

Say daily for 9 days:

+ In the name of the Father, and of the Son, and of the Holy Spirit. Amen.

I am the wheat of God, and am ground by the teeth of the wild beasts, that I may be found the pure bread of God. I long after the Lord, the Son of the true God and Father, Jesus Christ. Him I seek, who died for us and rose again. I am eager to die for the sake of Christ. My love has been crucified, and there is no fire in me that loves anything.

But there is living water springing up in me, and it says to me inwardly: "Come to the Father."

Amen

(Mention your request here…)

Followed by:
one Our Father, Hail Mary, and Glory be to the Father.

HYMNS TO OUR LORD

Twice in St. Ignatius's letters he breaks into rhythmic passages that have sometimes been interpreted as verse. Are they are ancient Christian hymns known to those he was addressing or are they St. Ignatius's own compositions? We do not know, but here they are!

Our One Physician

Both earthborn and spirit too;
Both uncreated and conceived;
God existing in flesh;
True life in death;
Both of Mary and of God;
Both possible and impossible,
Even Jesus Christ our Lord.

~St. Ignatius to the Ephesians 7

Him Who is Above All Time

Eternal and intangible,
For us made visible,
Who nothing can pierce or maim,
For us accepted pain;
Choosing to endure,
Our salvation to secure.

~St. Ignatius to Polycarp 3

SAINT IGNATIUS'S LETTER TO THE ROMANS

From the *Ante-Nicene Christian Library*, Volume I,
edited by Alexander Roberts and James Donaldson.
(Lightly edited and modernized.)

G REETINGS
*From Ignatius,
who is also called Theophorus,*

*To the Church which has obtained mercy,
through the majesty of the Most High Father,
and Jesus Christ, His only-begotten Son;
to the Church which is beloved and enlightened
by the will of Him that wills all things
which are according to the love of our God Jesus Christ;
the church which also presides in the chief place
in the district of the Romans —
worthy of God,
worthy of honor,
worthy of the highest happiness,
worthy of praise,
worthy of obtaining her every desire,
worthy of being deemed holy,
and which is first in love,
which is named from Christ,
and from the Father.*

Greetings in the name of Jesus Christ,
the Son of the Father:
to those who are united,
both according to the flesh and spirit,
to every one of His commandments;
to those who are filled inseparably
with the grace of God,
and are purified from every strange taint,
I wish abundance of happiness,
in Jesus Christ our God.

I. AS A PRISONER, I HOPE TO SEE YOU.

My prayers to God that I might live to see your most worthy faces in the flesh have been granted, and even more than I requested; for I now hope to greet you in the very chains of a prisoner of Christ Jesus, if indeed it be the will of God that I be thought worthy of reaching my journey's end.

For things have made an admirable beginning, if I may only obtain grace to cling to my lot without hindrance until the end. For I am afraid of your love, in case it should do me an injury. For it is easy for you to accomplish what you wish to do; but it is going to be difficult for me to reach God, unless you spare me from your intervention.

II. DO NOT SAVE ME FROM MARTYRDOM.

For it is not my desire for you to please men, but to please God, as you usually do. For I shall never have another such opportunity of getting to God; nor will you, if you shall now be silent, ever be entitled to the honor of a better piece of work. For if you are silent concerning me, I shall become God's; but if your love is only for my poor mortal flesh, I shall again have to run my race.

Pray, then, do not seek to confer any greater favor upon me than that I be sacrificed to God while the altar is still prepared. Then, being gathered together in love, you may sing praise to the Father, through Christ Jesus, that God has deemed me, the bishop of Syria, worthy to be sent for from the east unto the west. How good it is to be setting out from the world towards God, that I may rise again in His dawn!

III. PRAY RATHER THAT I MAY ATTAIN TO MARTYRDOM.

You have never envied any one; you have instructed many. Now I desire that this may be confirmed by your conduct, just as you have taught others. I would only ask you to request on my behalf both inward and outward strength, that I may be resolved in will, not only in words; and that I may not merely be called a Christian, but really be found to be one. (For once I have been found a Christian in reality, I may also be called one, and may be deemed faithful when I shall no longer appear to the world.)

Nothing visible is eternal. "For the things which are seen are temporal, but the things which are not seen are eternal." For our God, Jesus Christ, now that He is with the Father, is all the more revealed in His glory. Christianity is not a thing of speech or silence only, but of manifesting greatness in the face of the hatred of the world.

IV. ALLOW ME TO FALL A PREY TO THE WILD BEASTS.

I am writing to the Churches, to impress on them all that I am truly willing to die for God, unless you hinder me. I beseech you not to show such untimely goodwill towards me. Suffer me to become food for the wild beasts, for they can enable me to reach God. I am the wheat of God; let me be ground by the teeth of the wild beasts, that I may become the pure bread of Christ.

Better yet, entice the wild beasts to become my tomb, and leave nothing of my body; so that when I have fallen asleep, I may be no trouble to anyone. When the world shall not see even so much as my body, then shall I truly be a disciple of Christ.

Entreat Christ for me, that by these instruments I may be found a sacrifice to God. I do not, as though a Peter or a Paul, issue commandments to you. They were apostles; I am but a condemned man: they were free, while I am still a slave. (But if I suffer, Jesus shall make me his Freedman, and I shall rise again emancipated in Him.) For now, my chains are teaching me to have done with worldly desires.

V. I DESIRE TO DIE.

From Syria to Rome I already fight with beasts both by land and sea, by night and day, being bound to half-a-score of fierce leopards (I mean a band of soldiers) who, even when they receive gratuities, show themselves all the worse. But their injuries help me to make progress in my discipleship; "yet I am not thereby justified."

How I look forward to the real beasts that are prepared for me! I pray they may be eager. I will entice them to devour me speedily, and not deal with me as with some, whom, out of fearfulness, they have not touched. But if they be unwilling to assail me, I will compel them to do so. Pardon me in this: I know what is for my benefit.

Now I begin to be a disciple. Let no power, visible or invisible, grudge me that I should reach Jesus Christ. Let fire and the cross; packs of wild beasts; lacerations, breakings and dislocations of bones; cutting off of members; shattering of the whole body—let all the dreadful torments of the devil come upon me: only let me win through to Jesus Christ!

VI. BY DEATH I SHALL ATTAIN TRUE LIFE.

All the pleasures of the world, and all the kingdoms of this earth, shall profit me nothing. It is better for me to die on behalf of Jesus Christ, than to reign over all the ends of the earth. "For what shall a man profit, if he gain the whole world, but lose his own soul?" Him alone do I seek, who died for us: Him alone do I desire, who rose again for our sake.

The birth pangs are upon me; bear with me, brethren: do not bar me from living, do not wish for me to be stillborn. I desire to belong only to God; do not give me back to the world. Suffer me to reach pure light: only once I have shall I be a true man. Permit me to imitate of the passion of my God.

If anyone has Him within himself, let him understand what I desire, and let him have sympathy for me, knowing how I am straitened.

VII. REASON FOR DESIRING TO DIE.

The prince of this world hopes to carry me away, and corrupt my resolution towards God. Pray let none of you in Rome help him; rather be on my side, that is, on the side of God. Do not speak of Jesus Christ, and yet set your desires on the world. Do not begrudge me my fate; not even if I should exhort you when present with you, do not be persuaded to listen to me, but rather give credit to what I now write to you.

For, although I am alive and well as I write this to you, I passionately yearn for my death. My Desire has been crucified; there is left in me no spark of fondness for worldly things, but living water wells up inside me and whispers, "Come to the Father."

I have no delight in corruptible food, nor in the pleasures of this life. I desire the bread of God, the heavenly bread, the bread of life, which is the flesh of Jesus Christ, the Son of God, who is of the seed of David and Abraham; and I desire the drink of God, namely His blood, which is incorruptible love and eternal life.

VIII. BE YOU FAVOURABLE TO ME.

I wish for no more of what men call life. And my desire shall be fulfilled if you consent. Be willing, then, that you also may have your desires fulfilled. I entreat you in this brief letter; believe me. Jesus Christ will reveal to you that I speak the truth. He is the mouth altogether free from falsehood, by which the Father truly speaks.

Pray for me, that I may attain the object of my desire. I have not written to you according to the flesh, but according to the will of God. If I suffer, you have wished me well; but if I am rejected, you have hated me.

IX. PRAY FOR THE CHURCH IN SYRIA.

Remember in your prayers the Church in Syria, which now has God for its shepherd, instead of me. Jesus Christ alone will oversee it, and your love will also aid it. But as for me, I am ashamed to be counted one of them; for indeed I am not worthy, as being the very last of them, an embryo born before time. But I have obtained mercy to be somebody, if I shall attain to God.

I salute you in spirit; and the Churches that have

received me in the name of Jesus Christ—and not as a mere passer-by—also send their love. (For even those churches which were not near to my bodily route have travelled to accompany me, city to city.)

X.   **CONCLUSION**
Now I write these things to you from Smyrna, to send by the hands of the praiseworthy Ephesians. There is also with me, along with many others, Crocus, one dearly beloved by me.

As to those who have gone before me from Syria to Rome for the glory of God, I believe that you are acquainted with them. Make known to them that I am near at hand. For they are all worthy, both of God and of you; and it is becoming that you should set their minds at ease as you can.

I have written these things to you,
on the twenty-third day of August.
Fare you well unto the end,
in the patience of Jesus Christ.
Amen.

THE MARTYRDOM OF SAINT IGNATIUS

From the *Ante-Nicene Christian Library*, Volume I,
edited by Alexander Roberts and James Donaldson.
(Lightly edited and modernized.)

I. IGNATIUS'S DESIRE FOR MARTYRDOM.

At the time when Trajan had not long since succeeded to the empire of the Romans, Ignatius, the disciple of John the apostle, a man in all respects of an apostolic character, governed the church of the Antiochians with great care.

Having with difficulty escaped the former storms of the many persecutions under Domitian—inasmuch as, like a good pilot, by the helm of prayer and fasting, by the earnestness of his teaching, and by his constant spiritual labor, he resisted the flood that rolled against him—he feared only lest he should lose any of those who were deficient in courage, or apt to suffer from their simplicity.

Therefore he rejoiced over the tranquil state of the church, when the persecution ceased for a little time, but was grieved that he had not yet, himself, attained to a true love of Christ, nor reached the perfect rank of a disciple. For he inwardly reflected that the confession which is made by martyrdom would bring him into a yet more intimate relation to the Lord.

Therefore, continuing a few years longer with the church, and, like a divine lamp, enlightening every one's understanding by his expositions of the Holy Scriptures, he at length attained the object of his desire.

II. IGNATIUS IS CONDEMNED BY TRAJAN.

For Trajan, in the ninth year of his reign, being lifted up with pride after the victory he had gained over the Scythians and Dacians, and many other nations, decided that the religious body of the Christians were yet wanting to complete the subjugation of all things to himself. Therefore, threatening them with persecution unless they should agree to worship dæmons, as did all other nations, he compelled all who were living godly lives either to sacrifice to idols or die.

Therefore the noble soldier of Christ, Ignatius, being in fear for the church of the Antiochians, was, in accordance with his own desire, brought before Trajan (who was at that time staying at Antioch, but was in haste to set forth against Armenia and the Parthians).

And when Ignatius was set before the emperor Trajan, that prince said to him, "Who are you, wicked wretch, who sets yourself to transgress our commands, and persuades others to do the same, so that they should miserably perish?"

Ignatius replied, "No one ought to call Theophorus wicked; for all evil spirits have departed from the servants of God. But if, because I am an enemy to these spirits, you call me wicked in respect to them, I quite agree with you; for inasmuch as I have Christ the King of heaven within me, I destroy all the devices of these evil spirits."

Trajan answered, "And who is Theophorus?"

Ignatius replied, "He who has Christ within his breast."

Trajan said, "Do we not then seem to you to have the gods in our mind, whose assistance we enjoy in fighting against our enemies?"

Ignatius answered, "You are in error when you call the dæmons of the nations gods. For there is but one God, who made heaven, and earth, and the sea, and all that are in them; and one Jesus Christ, the only-begotten Son of God, whose kingdom may I enjoy."

Trajan said, "Do you mean him who was crucified under Pontius Pilate?"

Ignatius replied, "I mean Him who crucified my sin, with him who was the inventor of it, and who has condemned and cast down all the deceit and malice of the devil under the feet of those who carry Him in their heart."

Trajan said, "Do you then carry within you Him that was crucified?"

Ignatius replied, "Truly so; for it is written, 'I will dwell in them, and walk in them.'"

Then Trajan pronounced sentence as follows: "We command that Ignatius, who affirms that he carries about within him Him that was crucified, be bound by soldiers, and carried to the great city Rome, there to be devoured by the beasts, for the gratification of the people."

When the holy martyr heard this sentence, he cried out with joy, "I thank You, O Lord, that You have vouchsafed to honor me with a perfect love towards You, and have made me to be bound with iron chains, like Your Apostle Paul."

Having spoken thus, he then, with delight, clasped the chains about him; and when he had first prayed for the church, and commended it with tears to the Lord, he was hurried away by the savage cruelty of the soldiers, like a distinguished ram, the leader of a goodly flock, that he might be carried to Rome, there to furnish food to the bloodthirsty beasts.

III. IGNATIUS SAILS TO SMYRNA.

Therefore, with great alacrity and joy, because of his desire to suffer, he came down from Antioch to Seleucia, from which place he set sail. And after a great deal of suffering he came to Smyrna, where he disembarked with great joy, and hastened to see the holy Polycarp, formerly his fellow-disciple, and now bishop of Smyrna. (For they had both, in old times, been disciples of St. John the apostle.)

Being then brought to him, and having communicated to him some spiritual gifts, and glorying in his bonds, Ignatius entreated of Polycarp to labor along with him for the fulfilment of his desire; earnestly indeed asking this of the whole church (for the cities and churches of Asia had welcomed the holy man through their bishops, and presbyters, and deacons, all hastening to meet him, hoping they might receive from him some spiritual gift). But above all, that, by means of the wild beasts, he might soon disappear from this world and be manifested before the face of Christ.

IV. IGNATIUS WRITES TO THE CHURCHES.

And these things he said, and testified to, extending his love to Christ so far as one who was about to secure heaven through his good confession. And to those who earnestly joined their prayers to his in regard to his approaching conflict—and to give a recompense to the churches, who came to meet him through their rulers— he sent letters of thanksgiving to them, which dropped spiritual grace, along with prayer and exhortation.

Because of which, seeing all men feeling so kindly towards him, and fearing lest the love of the brotherhood should hinder his zeal towards the Lord while a fair door of suffering martyrdom was opened to him, he wrote to the church of the Romans the epistle which is here attached [see page 138].

V. IGNATIUS IS BROUGHT TO ROME.

Having therefore, by means of this epistle, settled, as he wished, those of the brethren at Rome who were unwilling for his martyrdom; and setting sail from

Smyrna (for Christophorus was pressed by the soldiers to hasten to the public spectacles in the mighty city of Rome, so that, being given up to the wild beasts in the sight of the Roman people, Ignatius might attain to the crown for which he strove), he next landed at Troas.

Then, going on from that place to Neapolis, he went on foot by Philippi through Macedonia, and on to that part of Epirus which is near Epidaumus; and finding a ship in one of the seaports, he sailed over the Adriatic Sea, and entering from it on the Tyrrhene, he passed by the various islands and cities, until, when Puteoli came in sight, he was eager there to disembark, having a desire to tread in the footsteps of the Apostle Paul.

But a violent wind arising did not suffer him to do so, the ship being driven rapidly forwards; and, simply expressing his delight over the love of the brethren in that place, he sailed by.

Wherefore, continuing to enjoy fair winds, we were reluctantly hurried on in one day and a night, mourning as we did over the coming departure from us of this righteous man. But to him this happened just as he wished, since he was in haste as soon as possible to leave this world, that he might reach the Lord whom he loved.

Sailing then into the Roman harbor, and the unhallowed sports being just about to end, the soldiers began to be annoyed at our slowness, but the bishop joyfully yielded to their urgency.

VI.

IGNATIUS IS DEVOURED BY THE BEASTS.

They pushed forth therefore from the place which is called Portus; and (the fame of all relating to the holy martyr being already spread abroad) we met the brethren full of fear and joy; rejoicing indeed because they were thought worthy to meet with Theophorus, but struck with fear because so eminent a man was being led to death.

Now he enjoined some to keep silence who, in their fervent zeal, were saying that they would appease the people, so that they should not demand the destruction of this just one. He was immediately aware of this through the Spirit, and having saluted them all, he begged them to show a true affection towards him.

Having dwelt on this point at greater length than in his epistle, and having persuaded them not to envy him hastening to the Lord, he then, with all the brethren kneeling beside him, entreated the Son of God on behalf of the churches, that a stop might be put to the persecution, and that mutual love might continue among the brethren. After which, he was led with all haste into the amphitheater.

Then, he was immediately thrown in, according to the command of Cæsar given some time ago, for the public spectacles was just about to finish (for it was then a solemn day, as they deemed it, being that which is called the thirteenth in the Roman tongue, on which the people were accustomed to assemble in more than ordinary numbers).

Therefore, he was cast to the wild beasts close beside the temple, that by them the desire of the holy martyr Ignatius should be fulfilled, according to that which is written, "The desire of the righteous is acceptable to God," to the effect that he might not be troublesome to any of the brethren by necessitating the gathering of his remains (as he had in his epistle expressed a wish beforehand).

For only the harder portions of his holy remains were left, which were conveyed to Antioch and wrapped in linen, as an inestimable treasure left to the holy church by the grace which was in the martyr.

VII. IGNATIUS APPEARS IN A VISION.
Now these things took place on the thirteenth day before the Calends of January, that is, on the twentieth of December, Sura and Senecio being then the consuls of the Romans for the second time.

Ourselves having been eye-witnesses of these things, we spent the whole night in tears within the house. Having entreated the Lord, with bended knees and much prayer, that He would give us weak men full assurance respecting the things which were done, it came to pass, on our falling into a brief slumber, that some of us saw the blessed Ignatius suddenly standing by us and embracing us. Others beheld him again praying for us, and others still saw him dropping with sweat, as if he had just come from his great labor, and standing by the Lord.

When, therefore, we had with great joy witnessed these things, and had compared our several visions together, we sang praise to God, the giver of all good things, and expressed our sense of the happiness of the holy martyr.

Now we have made known to you both the day and the time when these things happened, that, assembling ourselves together according to the time of his martyrdom, we may have fellowship with the champion and noble martyr of Christ, who trod underfoot the devil, and perfected the course which, out of love to Christ, he had desired, in Christ Jesus our Lord; by whom, and with whom, be glory and power to the Father, with the Holy Spirit, for evermore!

Amen.

DON'T MISS RAZIM'S OTHER STORY:

DO CARPENTERS DREAM OF WOODEN SHEEP?

A FRIENDS IN HIGH PLACES SPIN-OFF

**THE STORY OF SAINT JOSEPH—
WITH A SCI-FI TWIST!**

Razim's staying overnight to help his friend Daniel, who's sick with leukaemia, but he's forgotten his phone! Lying awake after watching Bladerunner, Razim reads the only story he can find—about Joseph and Mary—only to fall asleep and find himself in futuristic Merillia.

In Merillia, his name is Cleopas, and his big brother, Jo, is considering an arranged marriage to a girl called Miryam. Soon, events are in motion that will change their lives—and the world—forever.

For anyone who feels over-familiar with the Holy Family's story after Christmas after Christmas of nativity plays, this imaginative re-telling thoroughly blows the dust off.

A standalone spin-off from Corinna Turner's 'Friends in High Places' series, it can be read on its own or in between books 1 and 2.

**TURN OVER TO READ THE
FIRST 2 CHAPTERS!**

DO CARPENTERS DREAM
OF WOODEN SHEEP?

CHAPTER 1: BEDTIME READING

"Oh…" Swearing under my breath, I fish around in my overnight bag, even though I have a crystal-clear memory of plugging the charger into my phone and leaving it on my window ledge at home. No phone for me tonight.

I wasn't very loud, but over on the bed, Daniel stirs slightly. "What's wrong, Razim?"

I stop rummaging in my bag and lie still on my wobbly camp bed, not wanting to disturb him. "Oh, nothing."

Daniel's particularly tired tonight and he doesn't press the issue. I hear his breathing deepen and slow as he falls asleep, but I don't feel sleepy yet. I should, 'cos I was here Monday night and I'll be here again next Monday and I can't believe how tiring it is having even two disrupted nights a week. But that's why I'm here, of course.

When Daniel had his first round of chemo his parents insisted on one of them staying with him in his room every night, in case he needed anything. Daniel swore—still does—that he doesn't need it, but after the morning when they found vomit in a lot of places it shouldn't be, and Daniel curled up freezing-cold in the middle of the floor halfway to the bathroom because he'd got too tired to crawl back into bed, they insisted.

But they were like zombies by the end and that really upset Daniel. So when his second round of chemo clashed with another Covid lockdown, I hatched a clever plan. Well, I thought so at the time. I could come and stay over two nights a week to give his mum and dad a break. And that way I'd get to see Daniel, despite the lockdown, because I'd count as a 'carer.'

It took a lot of persuading, with both sets of parents — we coaxed, we argued, we even begged — and then to my shame, I almost quit after the first time. I suppose I had this idea that we'd chat and have at least a bit of fun. I guess I wasn't really prepared for all the —

Over on the bed, Daniel stirs, making a slight retching sound. I leap up from the camp bed, grab the basin from the floor and hold it out. "Need this?"

"Ugh..."

Yep, he vomits.

"You done?" I ask at last, trying, as usual, to sound as though holding a basin of puke is no biggie.

"Think so." His head sinks towards his pajama sleeve so I put the bowl down quick, snatch a tissue and hastily wipe his chin. I've learned all sorts of little tricks for keeping the smell down. He's so pale, the brown skin of my hand contrasts sharply with his face. Coffee and Cream, my big brother Sayeed used to call us — and

157

not in a nice way—but when he saw Daniel after his first round of chemo he called us Coffee and Milksop. I pushed him over into a bush but then I couldn't run for it the way I usually would because Daniel wasn't up to it, so I got well-pounded. Daniel said I shouldn't have reacted but he also gave me a tissue for my nose so I forgave him.

"You gonna need this again, man?" I nod to the bowl.

Daniel shakes his head without lifting it. "Don't see how I can possibly have any more where that came from," he jokes weakly.

Too right. It's been particularly bad, tonight. We tried to watch *Bladerunner* after I arrived—well, after I'd showered and put on clean clothes to reduce the risk of transmitting anything to immune-suppressed Daniel— but Daniel puked through most of it. Ugh, he's fifteen, not much older than me, he shouldn't be this sick!

I barely managed to make myself come back, the second time, it was all such a shock. The vomiting. The stench. And just...seeing Daniel this weak and down. Unbearable. But I figured I wasn't much of a friend if I could let a bit of puke stop me helping out, and I *made* myself come back. And I'm glad. I mean, he's my best mate, but if he can't beat this leukemia, well, he could just be...gone...by the time this Covid-thing is all over.

"You're nearly done with the chemo, right?" I say, when his eyes don't close again immediately. "There're what, less than two weeks left?" Like we don't both know that, but it's the most cheerful thing I can think to say.

"Yep." He musters a smile.

Even with his weird new optimism about everything, a few times he's got so tired that he's just cried. Quiet, helpless weeping, like he simply can't help it. It's horrible. And I can tell he's ashamed when he gets like that, so I just talk cheerful, like crying's no big deal, and try to distract him from how awful he's feeling, but I don't feel like it works. Thankfully, he's not quite that tired tonight. Yet.

"And the Lockdown's easing on twenty-ninth March," I say. "So, just think, a few days to get your strength back, and we can go down to the park, get an ice cream, fly my hovercraft…" I got a remote-controlled hovercraft for Christmas, and Daniel hasn't had much chance to see it in action, yet. It knocks the socks off a remote control car or boat, the way it can just go straight down the bank and out onto the lake.

Daniel nods and smiles. "Well, if it's actually still in one piece!"

I laugh. "Yeah, okay, I pulled it apart and changed a few things, but I got it back together okay."

"Of course you did," murmurs Daniel. But then his smile fades. His hand rises to run over his bald head. "Wish it wasn't getting so hot—" He breaks off suddenly, his pale cheeks going slightly pink, the way they do when he feels like he's been grumbling. The new Daniel doesn't hold with grumbling.

I guess he's worried he won't want to wear a woolly hat, the way he did after his last course of treatment. I remember after his hair started falling out again, all couple of millimeters of it, how he just muttered, "Here we go again," and never said another word about it. I guess it bothers him more than he likes to let on.

"Ah, we'll be, like, a skinhead gang, man. It'll be cool."

Daniel shoots me a look, smiles a too-polite smile and closes his eyes.

Okay, that went down like a lead balloon. Guess you can't really have a skinhead 'gang' when only one of you is bald. I carry the stinking basin to the bathroom, empty it and rinse it out, getting it back to the room as fast as I can, just in case—but Daniel's sleeping quietly.

At least it sounds like the doctors are hopeful hitting it again this soon will put it into remission. They didn't really give him long enough to recover in between, but they said this was the only chance.

It will be worth it. If…

I sigh, stretch out on my cot, fold my arms behind my head and stare up at the ceiling. Tired or not, it's too early to sleep. I can't believe I forgot my phone. I'm an idiot.

I glance around the room. Beside Daniel's computer stands a pile of schoolbooks that he still tries to open occasionally because he doesn't want to get held back a year. No, thanks. I glance at the bedside table. Bible…nope, some sort of prayer book, er, nope…what's that one? I sit up and pick up a thin booklet and look at the cover. A handsome young man stands protectively over a beautiful young woman holding a baby. All with a similar brown skin tone to mine. I eye their features, trying to figure out what race they are, but I'm not sure. Something Middle Eastern, perhaps? Their noses are quite sharp.

The Tale of Joseph and Mary, says the heading. Hey, maybe it's fiction. That'd do. As long as it's not a romance. But Daniel's not into soppy stuff and it must be quite a manly romance, from the cover. I flop back on the camp bed and open the booklet.

Oh. Maybe it's not fiction. There's an 'introduction' by someone or other. I flick past it. Uh-oh. The first chapter begins with a Bible quote. Heck, it's another of Daniel's religious books, isn't it? He went super-religious after getting his diagnosis. It makes me kinda want to ditch him sometimes, when he really gets going, but even if we hadn't been friends since kindergarten, that light in his eye… It's scary as heck, but it fascinates me, too. I just wish I could figure out how he can be so flaming *happy* when he's in this fix.

I don't want to start rootling around the room for something else to read and wake Daniel, so I scan the quote. Okay, nothing terrifying. It just says something about 'a virgin engaged to a man whose name was Joseph, of the house of David. The virgin's name was Mary.' Guess that's Mary and Joseph on the cover.

Hang on…I turn the booklet over and read the back. Oh, okay. So this is about Maryam, mother of Jesus, or Isa as my parents would call him. And Joseph is her *husband*? I might have heard something about a Joseph, at Christmas time, but the penny hadn't dropped. Maryam was *married*? Wow. What sort of man would put up with his wife just getting mystically pregnant like that? I mean, *back then*? When I was little and my parents still took us to the mosque occasionally and even made us sit in some classes, I don't remember ever hearing about Joseph. What sort of man could be worthy to marry Maryam, Isa's *ammi*?

I turn back to the beginning and start reading. The story is way more exciting than I expected. Soon I'm well impressed with this Joseph guy. Maryam was lucky to have him. Except I guess Daniel would say it wasn't luck, right?

When, yawning, I put the booklet down rather later than I intended and plonk my head on the pillow, Joseph still strides through my mind, young and brave and reminding me a heck of a lot of Daniel—at least, the way he is now. That bewildering trust that I can't quite figure out. That freakish calm. Sounds like Joseph had it too.

I don't really have any problems in my life—may have thought I did once, but Daniel's illness has made it clear I don't have any real ones—but if I ever had problems like those characters in *Bladerunner*, or like Joseph and Maryam, or like Daniel...it would be nice to be all brave and peaceful. But how do they do it?

Yeah... Another yawn stretches my jaws. Be nice... But how...?

+

RAZIM'S DREAM

CHAPTER 2: THE BETROTHAL

"I can't believe you're going through with this." I raise my voice over the sound of a hover-bus passing too close over the top of our ancient domestic pod.

Jo carefully straightens the colorful wide sash that's been part of Merillian formal wear for centuries, even though it's falling out of use in favor of Imperial fashions, nowadays. "Why? It's traditional."

"Yeah, but you don't have *to anymore. That's a freedom the Empire actually has brought."*

Jo shoots me a look of amusement. "It's an arranged *marriage, little bro, not a* forced *marriage. Big diff. And it's not like the way it used to be done. All we're doing today is getting introduced. Then we get to know each other, and only then do we decide whether we want to go ahead and get married."*

"I still don't see why you don't just find a girl for yourself."

"Because the matchmaker has spent decades learning who's likely to be compatible with whom. So I might as well give this a try first, right?"

When he puts it like that, it doesn't sound so dumb, not if you're looking for marriage and no sordid messing around, which is definitely what my big brother is after. Some people use the info-xchange to find girlfriends, after all. Probably better to trust your future happiness to a person than to a machine.

"Well, I've got your back, whatever you decide."

He grins at me. "Thanks, Cleo." He fidgets with his sash again. He's more nervous than he's letting on.

"You look good," I tell him. "She'll swoon."

"Ah, very funny." But he looks fractionally more relaxed as he heads for the broken up-down conveyer. Not for the first time, as we trek downstairs, I wonder what it's like to live in a domestic pod where everything works. Jo swears that when I was very young, when Amma and Abba were both still alive and had recently moved here from Bethlasa, our pod was all in proper order, like other people's. But I don't remember. I barely even remember them. Jo's been keeping us with his woodcarving since forever.

At least now I'm old enough to have my hover-permit, I

can do delivery work and make some money too. Seeing that I'm rubbish at carving. I'm good at fixing things, but you have to be careful, showing serious skills. Imperial soldiers get a bounty for every conscript they sign up, which is why they get so rough about it—but if they sign up someone skilled, they get double. They don't need carpenters—wood goods are for decoration—but engineers? I'm better off delivering stuff, even if the pay is low.

Sealing the pod behind us, we climb into the hover-van I managed to scrape together enough to buy and we're off through the streets to the matchmaker's.

"Okay," I say, parking two doors down, under a lurid flickering neon sign. "Time to meet your fate."

"Very funny," says Jo. Sweating. Well, he decided to do this.

We keep a careful lookout for swipe-thieves, regional security forces, or imperial soldiers as we walk the short distance to the matchmaker's door. The first will beat you and take your valuables, the second will frisk you in a more official manner but make your stuff disappear just as fast, and the third might do either—or worse, conscript you on the spot.

In we go. The up-down here works, and soon we're being shown into the matchmaker's receiving room. Oh boy…the prospective bride is already here, standing between her elderly parents with her head bowed. They look old enough to drop off their perches any time, in fact. Is that why she's put herself up for an arranged marriage? If they've got nothing to leave her...well, it's hard for a woman to survive alone. Between Imperial taxes and the Regional Supreme Leader's whims and the dangerous streets... Well, that doesn't matter, if she's both nice and pretty. I guess Jo, being Jo, will only really care if she's nice. But I stare, trying to make out her face.

Jo stops and bows formally, so I do the same. Our traditions are getting forgotten fast, now we're part of the Empire, but not by Jo.

The bridal party bows as well, and finally the young woman looks up. Girl. The girl looks up. She's young, maybe sixteen, her skin smooth coffee perfection, her eyes dark and warm. And her poise...like a katachara dancer. And...and... something else about her. What is it?

Jo is staring at her as though he's been struck dumb, but the matchmaker is clearly used to this and begins some spiel of introduction that gives Jo time to pull himself together. Then I take tea with the matchmaker and the elderly parents of the bride—Joachim and Annei—while Jo goes into the matching chamber for private refreshments with the girl herself. Miryam, her name is. Her parents are sweet and kind and doddery, and embarrassingly enthusiastic about me— even though it's Jo who's going to be marrying their daughter if it all works out—and I'm not sorry when the hour is up.

Jo is silent as we take the up-down back to the lobby. It's up to me to keep an eye out for danger as we walk the short distance back to the hover-van. He settles into the seat silently, still staring into space.

166

"So?" Once my door is sealed to keep out the smog, I can't wait any longer. "What did you think of her?"

He turns his head slowly, like a man coming out of a dream, wonder in his eyes. "Did you ever…ever see anything so pure in all your life? Anyone so pure…"

Pure. Yes, that was it, the indefinable quality about Miryam. Purity. Not unlike my big brother, only—and I'd not have thought it possible—even more so. I glance at Jo's face. Oh yeah, it's a done deal, all right.

And three weeks later, Miryam and Jo become formally betrothed. Big surprise. Not.

AVAILABLE NOW
in paperback and eBook!

DON'T MISS THE REST OF THE SERIES!

FRIENDS IN HIGH PLACES 1: CARLO ACUTIS
The Boy Who Knew

"YOU HAVE LEUKEMIA."

Daniel's just received the worst news a teen can get. The adults in his life are crumbling under the shock. In desperation, he turns to his parish priest for help and is introduced to a boy his age, Carlo Acutis—who just happens to be dead.

Daniel's convinced the priest is wasting his time. But as he struggles to come to terms with his uncertain future an unlikely friendship develops between him and the holy dead boy—who may not be quite so dead after all.

The Boy Who Knew is the first title in Carnegie Medal nominee Corinna Turner's 'Friends in High Places' series. If you've always been interested in the saints but find dry biographies boring and hard to get through, this fast-paced story is for you.

"Powerful and inspiring."
SUSAN PEEK, author of the God's Forgotten Friends serie

"beautifully honest"
KARINA FABIAN, author of *Discovery*

FRIENDS IN HIGH PLACES 2: SAINT JOSEPH
Old Men Don't Walk to Egypt

FRIENDS, POPULARITY, BOYFRIEND, CHECK. HAPPINESS...?

Katie has everything she thinks she wants—friends, popularity, and a gorgeous athletic older boyfriend. But the more time she spends with Shaun, the more miserable she feels.

When freaky Daniel suggests Saint Joseph for her research project, her supposedly perfect life spirals out of control. Will the carpenter from Nazareth destroy everything she thinks matters—or give her even the things she didn't know she wanted?

Old Men Don't Walk to Egypt is the second book in the Friends in High Places series, but can be read on its own. The series is Parental Guidance since it contains some mature themes.

"Despite being beyond blessed as a Dominican Sister of Saint Joseph to be under his patronage, I always struggled most of all in getting to know St. Joseph as a flesh-and-blood person. Seeing him through Katie's eyes has had a beautiful and unexpected impact on my own relationship with him and—finally—I've found a friend and spiritual father in St. Joseph!"
SR. M. CATHERINE BLOOM, OP

FRIENDS IN HIGH PLACES 3: MARGARET OF CASTELLO
Child, Unwanted

NO ONE'S ADOPTING SCARFACE. I'M NOT THAT DUMB.

Abandoned by everyone in his life and scarred from a failed abortion attempt, Miri struggles to believe his new foster family could really want him.

When a devastating accident changes everything, all hope seems gone—until a young woman once equally unwanted starts visiting him in hospital.

Can 'Little Margaret' teach Miri that his life is still worth living, now more than ever?

The third book in the Friends in High Places series, *Child, Unwan*ted can be read as a standalone. The series is Parental Guidance since it contains some mature themes.

"An inspiration for all ages, but especially teens who find their lives lacking in comfort, physical beauty, and perhaps even paternal love... Child Unwanted *demonstrates the joy we can experience when we know God and accept His love for us."*
CYNTHIA T. TONEY, author of Catholic Press Association book award winner *The Other Side of Freedom*

ALL BOOKS IN THE SERIES AVAILABLE AS PAPERBACKS OR EBOOKS.

ACKNOWLEDGEMENTS

I'd like to thank G. M. Baker, Nancy Bechel, Karina Fabian, Marie C. Keiser, Sarah Robsdottir, and Andrea Rodgers for all their excellent editorial help—plus anyone I have forgotten!

Thanks to my parents for all their support, and to my Mum for her honest critiques.

And I must not forget Saint Ignatius of Antioch, the patron of this book—and last but the opposite of least, the Holy Spirit, who is responsible for it all.

ABOUT THE AUTHOR

Corinna Turner has been writing since she was fourteen and likes strong protagonists with plenty of integrity. Although she spends as much time as possible writing, she cannot keep up with the flow of ideas, for which she offers thanks—and occasional grumbles!—to the Holy Spirit. She is the author of over thirty books, including the Carnegie Medal Nominated I Am Margaret series, and her work has been translated into four languages. She was awarded the St. Katherine Drexel award in 2022.

She is a Lay Dominican with an MA in English from Oxford University and lives in the UK. She is a member of a number of organizations, including the Society of Authors, Catholic Teen Books, Catholic Reads, the Angelic Warfare Confraternity, and the Sodality of the Blessed Sacrament. She used to have a Giant African Land Snail, Peter, with a 6½" long shell, but now makes do with a cactus and a campervan.

Sign up for **free short stories** & **news** at:
www.UnSeenBooks.com

All Free/Exclusive content subject to availability.

www.ingramcontent.com/pod-product-compliance
Lightning Source LLC
Chambersburg PA
CBHW020127180626
46810CB00004B/1430